# All Flavors

## Also by Julie Barnes

*From the Depths: A Therapeutic Thriller*

# All Flavors

*Based on True Events*

## Julie Barnes

Foundation Books

All Flavors
Based on True Events

Published by
Foundation Books

Contact: JBarnesAuthor.com

ISBN: 978-0-9791476-8-5 (trade paperback)
ISBN: 978-0-9791476-0-9 (audiobook)
ISBN: 978-0-9791476-2-3 (ebook)

Interior and cover design by Marigold Emal
Cover art by Farras Raihan

Printed in the United States of America

To Beatrice Shea for your pure example
Noah, for your support
Shae, for your compassion
Karin, for a lifetime of friendship
Brody, for coming here as love

"I have deep faith that the principle of the universe will be beautiful and simple."
– Albert Einstein

"Sometimes it falls upon a generation to be great. You can be that great generation."
– Nelson Mandela

"We're all just walking each other home."
– Ram Dass

# CHAPTER 1

∞

I WONDERED IF we were flying over Texas. I thought about asking my mom, but she had a scrunched look on her face, like she didn't want to start crying again. When I told her that I needed to use the restroom, she looked at me with wide eyes.

She finally responded, "Oh! Yes. Come on, sweetie." Then we walked down the narrow aisle of the airplane to the small restroom.

We were on our way to Phoenix, but the trip was not a vacation. We received the news from Aunt Karin the day before while we were checking out at the store. Karin had called twice in a row, and then she left a message. After we finished paying for the groceries, Mom tried to push our cart with one hand as she listened to the message, and I had to grab the front of the cart before it hit a lady. We make a good team that way.

She moved us closer to the wall and dialed Karin's number. We stood near the area where shoppers push their full carts toward the exits, and people waited to buy cigarettes and lottery tickets.

"Bone, are you okay?" Mom asked. She often called Aunt Karin this funny name. They were very young when they started calling each other Bone. I thought it might be because they had both been skinny as little kids. Karin was not my biological aunt, but she was my mom's best friend and my Godmother. They were both LPNs, which Mom joked that it translated to "low paid nurse."

"What?" she asked Karin. "What? No, he's not! No!" And then she started screaming. She was crying and screaming really loud. I still knew that we were in the store, but she had apparently forgotten. My mom never likes to make a scene unless she needs to ask for the manager at a business. She's polite, but she tries to make sure that people treat us fairly. Everyone stared at her. There had been all this movement and busyness nearby, and then people were holding still to watch us. The checkout clerks in their blue aprons turned and looked our way.

"Please, no! Oh, no!" She cried even harder as she listened to Karin. I thought Karin's ear must hurt, but I had a feeling that she might be crying too.

"Yes, of course. I'm on the way!" Mom said. "I love you, Karin."

Now that she was off the phone, I wanted her to stop crying, but she covered her face with her hands and made this deep moaning sound. While she was taking a big breath, I touched her arm. I think she remembered where she was and that I was waiting.

"Let's go," she said, launching the cart forward. "We've got to go!"

So we hurried out the door and to the car, leaving the staring people behind. On the drive home, she leaned forward as if it would get us there faster. She was still crying, but in this more controlled way that let her see where she was going. I didn't want to ask her anything yet. I thought if I kept quiet and moved along with her that everything might stay under control.

"There's been an accident, Rylee," she told me as we turned down our street. She made a strange sound in her throat. "Brody. He got run over. And he…he didn't make it!" Then she started sobbing and couldn't speak.

Karin's little boy! It couldn't be true. I was just playing with Brody during their visit with us. I loved to look at the photo on our refrigerator of me holding Brody. He had green eyes and soft brown hair. Why would a one-year-old be allowed to die? He was brand new! That's when I felt everything start slipping away.

"No, Mom. No!" Tears began to flood my vision.

Brody had just been here, laughing in delight when I covered and uncovered my face. He had snuggled next to me when he got tired, his eyes slowly closing, draping us both with his pastel blanket. I wanted to save him, but it was too late.

When we arrived home we started packing, and my mom called the airlines and then her work. I filled eight bowls with a bunch of food and water for our cat and put her extra litter box out.

I heard Mom on the phone with Grandma Reilly. "Karin tried...to save Brody...and got run over too," she said, crying in between the words.

It seemed like we were in a bad dream that we would be able to wake up from soon. I wished that I could talk to Grandma Reilly. We had long conversations on the phone every weekend. She was my great-grandmother, and I was named after her, only Mom spelled my name differently.

I flinched as I saw an image in my mind of Karin darting in front of a speeding car, while Brody remained just beyond her reach. And now we were going there. I felt my stomach tighten up like it did at school whenever I had to speak in front of the class. What would I say to them?

Mom talked to Karin almost every night on our cell phone. They had a lot to talk about. She often told me stories about all the fun they had in Iowa when they were young. That was back when kids got to roam around free most of the day.

I had such trouble falling asleep, and soon we were up before sunrise to leave for the airport. In airports, it seems like time slows down, even though people are hurrying off to their destinations. If you worked in an airport, you might be able to set a timer and see if it's true, checking it with the time on a clock. If only we could go back in time to save someone. Grandma Reilly said that I'm philosophical. She was one of the people who treated me like an equal, even though I would only be turning nine on my next birthday.

We lived in Florida, so it was a long flight to Arizona. Karin's friend Deborah picked us up at the airport. As we drove through the dusty looking town, my eyes searched for glimpses of green, for fertile land.

Deborah spoke quietly about details of the accident. I learned that Karin's mom was ready to back out of her driveway. While she and Karin said goodbye, Brody had walked out of the garage along the other side of the car, climbing under it to reach for a ball. When Karin's mom started to back up, something stopped the car. Karin walked around it to see Brody pinned under the front wheel. She quickly tried to get his head away from the tire, but she didn't want to hurt his neck by pulling too hard. She stood and banged on the window, yelling for her mom to go forward. Karin crouched down, ready to move him, and that was when her mom backed up instead of driving forward. Karin's leg was run over, and Brody was still under the tire.

In all of these details, it seemed that somehow it should have been stopped. I wanted to change the scene so it would turn out that he was rescued, safely cuddled in Karin's arms. I felt sick. The motion of the car made me feel like throwing up.

Karin held Brody until the paramedics took him from her. She had been walking around on her hurt leg, holding Brody against her while he struggled for breath. A helicopter came to lift him away to the hospital, but Karin had to ride in an ambulance. Even though they hooked him up to machines for a little while, Brody died at the hospital. Karin had called us on her way back home from the hospital with her husband. John had been at work when the accident occurred.

Deborah said that Karin was in shock and that she kept insisting she needed my mom. Her leg was bruised but not broken. All of this had happened while we were picking out groceries at the store. No wonder my mom had screamed and cried. And now, my chest felt like it needed to break open and let out a volcano of screams.

We finally pulled up to the curb in front of Karin's house. The accident had taken place in her mother's driveway, so we didn't have to walk by where it happened. As we gathered our bags, Karin came limping out of the house and across the lawn.

"Andie! Oh, Andie!" she cried as she grabbed my mom. They hugged each other tightly, beginning to cry together.

"I'm so very, very sorry," Mom told her. "I wish I could change it."

Karin reached out and pulled me into their hug. It kind of hurt my ribs, but it felt good to feel something else so strong. "I love you, Rylee," she said. Her face was shiny with tears.

"I love you too, Aunt Karin. I'm really sorry about Brody." My voice was muffled by their close bodies.

We made it inside, where several people sat around the kitchen table. They all had puffy eyes. I saw Karin's daughter Fay in the living room, hunched in front of the TV. I went over and sat down next to her. She was only four, and I thought she probably needed another kid to be with her. She threw her arms around me and we fell sideways, rolling on the thick carpet.

"Do you want to go in my room?" she whispered. She took my hand and led me to her pink butterfly room. We sat on the canopy bed, and she picked up one of her stuffed animals, a purple lamb. She handed me a soft yellow rabbit. "Let's play," she told me.

We danced our animals around and made them talk to each other. It didn't seem like too long ago when I had played this way. But it felt stiff, even though I was trying to be creative for her sake. I couldn't get rid of the swollen feeling of what was happening around us. It ached in my chest. Fay had dark circles under her eyes, and it seemed like she was trying too hard, rather than enjoying herself. I found out later that she had seen the accident and that she had tried to prevent it.

Brody had woken up from the couch where Karin had laid him down asleep after their ride home. Karin's mom had been frantic about leaving quickly because she had lost her purse while they were out. Karin stood beside the driver's window, telling her mom to calm down, that everything would be okay. Brody had walked outside during this interaction, bumped into the ball, and crawled under the car to reach for it. Fay tried to alert them that Brody had gone under the car, pulling on her mom's shirt to get her attention, but they didn't recognize what she was saying. The noise of the car and the urgent conversation were too loud for her young voice to be understood. The accident was no one's fault.

Fay mentioned only one thing to me about it. The rabbit and the lamb were right in the middle of having their picnic. "There was…lots of red on Mama," she said quietly, and then she hugged the lamb to her cheek and closed her eyes. I didn't want to say anything to her about it. Four was old enough to be extremely frightened by what she'd seen, and there was no reason to take her back through it.

After Fay was asleep that evening, a few women sat in the living room with Karin. Mom was next to her on the couch when Karin suddenly leaned forward, waving her arms around. "Come here!" she cried. "Brody, please!" She slid onto the floor and pressed her forehead into the carpet. Mom knelt down and put her arms around her, and John hurried out from the kitchen to join them.

I didn't think that anyone in the living room was going to be able to really help Karin. I felt like we were intruding, looking into a deep place that only she had gone. You could tell that people didn't know exactly what to say to her, because they often paused, seeming to search for the right words. Every now and then, Karin looked hopeful that they might save her, and then her eyes would wander off, as if she were still seeing the unthinkable.

I slowly got up and walked to the guest room where we were staying, across the hall from Brody's room. Hanging on his closed door was a sign with his name written in colorful letters.

How could they face each new day after something like this? There were so many mornings ahead, and the loss of him was too much. I thought about how I'd felt when my dog had been hit by a car while she chased a rabbit. I was devastated. Each day, I would wake up and not remember for just a few seconds that Rosie was gone. It seemed so disrespectful to have a life end that way, bunched on a curb with cars rushing past.

My mom had also cried on and off for days because Rosie had been with her a long time. It had taken her a while to afford to have Rosie flown to us from Phoenix when my dad said he didn't want her anymore. Mom insisted that he not give her to anyone else, that she would be able to save enough money. Rosie used to lie next to my mom's pregnant belly, so she knew me from the start. I wanted to somehow keep Rosie, but Mom had said that we needed to bury her.

I wondered if Brody's funeral would be anything like what we did for Rosie. We wrote her name on a stone and put the date she was born and the date she had died. Then we shared what we loved about her. I said that I would miss how she could fetch. Not many dogs could fetch so well, bringing it right back to you for more. Rosie's favorite thing to fetch was a Frisbee. She could jump and twist around while up in the air to catch it. She was very special to me. And I loved how she warmed up my side and put her paw on me when we rested together.

We moved away from that duplex to another place, so I'm not sure if Rosie's stone is there anymore. I still miss her, even though we got a new pet.

# CHAPTER 2

∞

THE FIVE DAYS that we were in Phoenix seemed to blur together. I stayed out of the way, like most kids do during grown-up events. Two days before the funeral, Karin asked my mom to go into Brody's room with her. She hadn't gone back in there yet. I was in the guest room, but I could hear them talking. They were supposed to be picking out what he would wear for the funeral. I knew that meant forever, his final outfit.

It was quiet when they first went in. I imagined Karin staring at his crib and his toys. "I want him," she said slowly. "I want him so much. He can't be gone, Andie. This isn't real! Look, his pillow. His pillow! It...ohh. It smells just like him!"

Then she started speaking faster and louder. "He's going to need his blanket! He has to have it. Wait! Maybe he should wear this shirt. He looks so good in this one. So much older. And he'll need diapers. We always need extra diapers. And what about shoes? Does he need shoes? He's going to need his shoes!"

Karin sounded like she was never going to be able to slow down again.

Mom said something too softly for me to hear, and then Karin started crying hard. They walked out of Brody's room a few minutes later, and then they left for the funeral home. Karin insisted that she would be the one to take his clothes there, even though Mom and Deborah volunteered to do it.

I didn't like to make small talk, especially with people I barely knew, so I waited in the guest room while they were gone. I wished that Fay hadn't left, but another friend had taken her for the afternoon. She needed a break.

∞

The day of the funeral, I ended up sitting alone because Mom and Karin were late coming into the chapel. John had told Karin that it might be helpful to look at Brody one last time. The small white casket would be closed during the ceremony, but the funeral home allowed a family visitation in a different room. I stood with them outside that room while they talked about going in there. On the door was a gold sign with his name engraved in fancy letters. It didn't look right to be on this door, as if there was a grand way to present a child's death.

Mom went in with Karin, who made a quick turn and walked right back out. Karin hurried by me saying, "That's not him, not him!" It was probably no way to see anyone for the last time. I wouldn't want my mom looking at me in a casket. They stayed in the bathroom for quite a while.

At the beginning of the funeral, they showed a video with photos and film clips of Brody, starting from when he was born. While you watched him grow older, songs were playing. They were Brody's favorite songs, but they weren't baby songs. Many of the film clips showed him dancing, even before he could walk well. A song would begin, and then he would stop in place and listen closely. His head would start moving from side to side, and he'd lift one arm up and down, as if he was trying to snap his fingers to the beat. He'd bend at the knees and swing his hips around. It was so unusual, because you could tell he was really concentrating. That little guy loved music. On the paper that they handed to everyone at the funeral, it read "Dancing in Heaven" under his photograph.

After the funeral, I heard people whispering about God, asking why God would allow this tragedy, and saying that no parent should ever have to go through such a thing. They were absolutely right. I had some questions about this, too. I wanted to talk to Grandma Reilly.

It was not easy for my mom to say good-bye to Karin. They held each other, and Mom rocked her a little, like she did to me when I felt sad. Mom was good at it, maybe that's why she became a nurse. She could help someone feel better without doing a whole lot. But I could tell that Mom was upset and needing relief. I knew how she was feeling without her even saying anything to me. She probably wanted to fix everything, as usual, only this time it was impossible.

Karin's brother drove us to the airport. My mom told me that Tim was the brother she'd never had, since she had known him most of her life. I could tell that he felt the same way about her. He helped us take our luggage to the check-in area, and then he gave us both a hug. He had a terrific laugh, like bubbles quickly rising. He told Mom to call him anytime, for anything. Tim lived in Iowa, so we could visit him when we went back there.

We dozed on and off during the flight, because the time change still had us mixed up. I was relieved to be back in my own bed. I needed to feel cozy. It was not easy to get comfortable, though. I kept thinking of how Karin and her family were going to be sad and then having to walk by Brody's room day after day. How many people all over the world were sad about losing someone they loved? Especially if they had died unexpectedly. Brody was just here, and then he was gone in a flash like a quick strike of lightning, brilliant in his short time.

I knew that it took my mom a while to feel better after her mom died in her arms from lung cancer. Brody was a baby, though. It didn't make any sense. What was God thinking? Did God even care that Karin had thrown up from crying so hard? That John's only son had been taken from him? That Fay had to watch as her brother was hurt, and see her parents struggling through grief? I needed answers.

I learned about God by listening and watching. Mom used to be married to my step dad, who was a born-again Christian. His first wife took his kids far away from us, and he was never the same after that. Mom tried to make their marriage work, going to see counselors and staying with him even when he got mad, but they ended up getting divorced. I miss having the big family that we had.

Mom agreed to let my brother Noah live with him for part of the year. My real dad lives in Phoenix with his wife and two other daughters. He doesn't really call me or think of me. Mom said that he loves me; he just can't express his emotions. But if he loved me, then I would know it. They got divorced when I was only a baby, although I'm not sure why. I figured that if he ignored me like he did, then he couldn't have been very kind to my mom. I tried not to think of it too much because it made me feel sad in an empty way. Whenever I saw a girl having fun with her dad, I wondered what it would be like to have a dad love me.

So, I knew a few things about the born-again Christian version of God, the regular Christian version, the Catholic version, and the Jewish version. I was starting to learn about other types of religious people: Buddhist, Hindu, Muslim, and some that I hadn't even heard about before. Grandma Reilly and I talk about these things. Grandma answers all my questions and gives me real answers. She has experienced a lot in ninety years. I know that most religions believe that their way is the right and only way to heaven, that they alone have a special relationship with God that outsiders don't have. Grandma told me that more wars were started over religious differences than any other reason throughout all of history. I knew this meant that something wasn't working, but what was it?

It might be like the groups in school. If you're one of the outsiders, it's pretty hard to get in unless you act like they do and go along with their rules. There are some kids in my school that make fun of other kids who don't have the nicest clothes. They've called me names before, but I figured out with Grandma's help that if I smile to myself a little as I walk away, without saying anything back, they usually leave me alone. I also make sure they don't see me looking hurt, because that makes them crazy for more.

Grandma Reilly lived in Iowa, so we couldn't just drop in to see her. I planned to call her in the morning. Mom said that we would have moved back to Iowa to be closer to her after our divorce, but her adoptive brother still lived there, and she didn't want to relive her childhood. There seemed to be a lot of painful memories floating around in the world.

# CHAPTER 3

∞

WHEN I WOKE up, my mom was having a cup of coffee on the little patio off the back of our apartment. I liked to sit there and look toward the lake where the herons and other graceful birds hunted for food. We lived on the second floor of the apartment building, so we had a nice view. The bright sun promised another hot Florida day. Mom said that it was like living in a terrarium during the rainy season. School was almost over for the year, and then the real heat would begin.

"Good morning, sweetie," Mom said as I gave her a hug. She looked like she had been doing some deep thinking. "Did you sleep well?" she asked, smoothing the hair off my forehead. I liked her soft hands.

"Yeah, I think so." I stretched my arms, trying to wake up more. Maybe I had jet lag. I felt fuzzy-headed, as if part of me was still in Phoenix.

"We can call Grandma when you're more awake. She already called this morning." Mom looked across the field, then she picked up her cup and her journal to go inside with me. Our cat weaseled her way around our ankles to get onto the patio. Mittens liked to watch all the wildlife, too.

I was so glad that Grandma was waiting to talk to me. She always seemed to have a way of knowing when we needed her. Once she called after I fell off my bike and sprained my wrist. Another time she called the day that my mom told me about the divorce with my step dad. Mom didn't tell Grandma Reilly about the problems they were having until it was all over. She said that she never liked to worry Grandma. I didn't think that anything could worry Grandma. She might become concerned, but she never worried. She said worrying was putting negative ideas into motion.

I read that whenever you thought about an experience, your body went through the same reaction that it did the first time it happened to you. So you ended up having it happen to you all over again whenever you thought about it. The article said that stress is very hard on the body. Stress never feels good in my body, that's for sure. And if you worried about something in the future, you lived out the stress of it before anything had even happened yet. What a thing to do to yourself.

Grandma sent me interesting articles and links to websites that she found on the Internet. She hadn't wanted to get a computer until my mom finally convinced her that there would be a whole world of libraries at her fingertips. We loved to go to the library. Mom still read books to me, even though I had been reading on my own for several years. I didn't want other kids to know, but I liked reading the dictionary. Someone had to think up each and every word, and there were some zany ones in there that I bet I would never hear anyone use.

Grandma told me that words were really just labels, that our full thoughts were not easily put into words. She said a long time ago people decided to let different sounds have their own meaning, but our thoughts were much more than the sounds we made.

My mom used to have a round label gun that clicked out strips of letters that you could stick on things. You could go around labeling everything. I'd carefully feel the letters while my eyes were closed, trying to find out if I could read the words like Braille. I thought it would be neat to learn how to read Braille.

There was a blind man that my mom used to work with who needed someone to help him at home. She told me about his books of Braille and how his fingers moved quickly over the rows of raised dots. He wasn't blind his whole life, so he remembered colors. But how would you explain a color to someone who had never seen anything? They would probably read their Braille books about lush green fields and red sunsets. What would they imagine it all looked like? How could you explain what the sun was to them? A star...hmm, not enough information. A giant ball of fiery gas hanging in the sky? Now, that sounded pretty far-fetched.

And what about the eyes of other creatures, like cats? What if cat's eyes could actually perceive more than human eyes can see? There could be more things going on around us that we just aren't able to view with our kind of eyes.

Sometimes my questions never stopped. My mom said that I was inquisitive and that I usually went off on tangents. That's the thing about talking to adults, you needed to have a big vocabulary to understand what they meant a lot of the time.

Grandma Reilly's voice was great to hear. "Well, hello, Rylee," she said. "And how are you doing after such a journey?" She often used old-fashioned sounding expressions, which I usually understood.

"Oh, Grandma. I really need to talk to you. I've been having some trouble with things." I walked quickly into my bedroom and closed the door because I didn't want my mom to hear me. She already had enough to think about.

"Sweetheart, that was so very unexpected. I've been praying for Karin's family, and of course for you and your mother and Noah." Grandma was good at praying, because she'd had a lot of practice. "And how is Fay doing with it all?"

"Well, she was sort of blank. And not acting like a kid her age should act. I don't understand! It doesn't make *any* sense that God let this happen!"

"No, something like this does not make sense," she replied.

"This makes me mad, Grandma. I'm really mad about it! There's no way that God should've let this happen! Brody was just a baby! Karin tried to save him, but the car ran her over too. And Fay saw the whole thing!"

"Darling, please take a deep breath. I understand that you're upset. You'll have many emotions about this in the days to come, but don't give up on God. Just concentrate on healing thoughts for the family. Imagine Karin and Fay and John being happy. Wish them peace and good rest, and believe it will happen. Try to hold on to those thoughts for them, and for yourself. Expect God to take care of everyone."

"Um, Grandma? How can I expect God to do that after what happened? God isn't very nice at all!" I didn't like to be rude, but I was still mad.

"Rylee, I'm going to share many things with you soon. But I want you to be ready for it, so I'll wait until you're not angry. It won't explain what happened. I can't offer words to do that. It will help to explain our real part in life. Just be easy in your thoughts as much as you can be right now. Try to choose good things to think about as often as you can."

I heard my mom lightly knocking on the door. "Sweetie? Tell Grandma that I'll call her this weekend, okay? You can still finish up, but we need to go to the store soon." This was her way of also saying not to use too many cell phone minutes. Using the regular phone line was even more expensive to talk to someone far away. We did that one month and it really put a damper on the grocery buying. I had to wait for weeks before I could have any ice cream.

"Grandma, Mom says that she'll call you this weekend. I guess I need to go now. But will you tell me one more thing? Do you think God could have stopped this and didn't?"

"No, I don't believe that God would ever choose to let anyone be harmed. But people don't always understand the way that life works, so they sometimes blame God." I heard the creak of her old rocking chair, where she rocked slowly, tapping one foot in rhythm. "I love you dearly. It is always such a pleasure to visit with you, Rylee."

That was my cue. "Oh, but the pleasure was all mine." I knew she was smiling, too. This was the routine at the end of our conversations. "I love you, Grandma. And I'll talk to you soon! Bye-bye." I set the phone aside and leaned back on my bed.

I sure wished we lived closer. We could share afternoon tea together every day, because that was what we always did when we were with her. She would get out her finest tea set, and we would have vanilla cookies and lemon tea. She treated everyone like a royal guest, right there in her small apartment. That was probably why she had so many friends. On holidays, she usually received over forty greeting cards, even though she had outlived most of her same-age friends.

And she liked to joke about her age, saying: "I've got one foot in the grave and the other one on a banana peel." Then she would smile with that sparkle in her bright blue eyes. I wanted to be just like her when I grew up.

# CHAPTER 4

∞

MY MOM WORKED many hours to pay our bills. I usually stayed at school in their child care program while she was at work, and sometimes I'd get picked up after school by my friend Ashley's mom, who had watched me the previous summer. My brother spent the summers with his dad and grandparents. We always missed Noah, so we called him on the phone every other day. I asked Mom to let me stay home alone, but she said that I was too young. I liked being with Ashley, except for the fact that she talked a lot. It was difficult to have your own thoughts when someone was going on and on. It made me a little tired out.

But we didn't have any family nearby anymore who might help us. For family, we had Noah, and Great-Grandma Reilly and her son, my grandpa in Iowa. Mom was adopted, so she also had biological family. She had found them a long time ago and moved to Orlando to live by them. They keep in touch, but not as often because they moved away from Florida. Her biological mother, Sarah, is very sweet. She's always helping people in her community, but some of the things she talked about worried me.

I remember Grandma Sarah reading Bible stories. She told me not to commit sins because sinners might go to hell forever, which started my wondering about hell, where it was located and what went on there all day. Grandma Sarah told my mom something troubling when Mom asked her what she thought about Grandma Reilly's religious beliefs. She said that Grandma Reilly would not get to go to heaven because she wasn't a born-again Christian. But she didn't even know Grandma Reilly, who went regularly to her own church. If Grandma wasn't allowed in heaven, then I knew that I didn't stand a chance. All of this had left me feeling confused and anxious about the idea of God.

Grandma Reilly had a challenging childhood. When she was only four months old, her mom died. She had older brothers, but her father decided that he couldn't take care of a baby. He remarried soon after sending Grandma Reilly to live with her grandmother. When Grandma was only fifteen, her grandmother died. It was the saddest moment in her life. They were very poor, so she quit school in eighth grade because she would be on her own, and how would she afford anything? It was during the time of the Great Depression, so there were many starving families and few jobs. She always said that she wished she could have stayed in school. She finally found a job and rented a room, making her way early into the adult world.

When she was eighteen, she met her husband and got married. Her son was born when she was twenty. Grandma's husband was a bossy guy who liked other women and drinking, but Grandma stayed with him until her son was an adult. She said that she did it for him. Mothers did a lot of things for their kids that the kids didn't even know about.

Grandma finally divorced her husband, and she began working at the telephone company, back when operators had to plug thick cables into metal panels to make each connection so everyone could talk to each other. She was in charge of a lot of people. She retired when she was in her sixties, and she had saved enough money to do what she'd always dreamed of doing, seeing the world!

Mom was my age then, and she couldn't wait for Grandma to get back from her trips to places like Greece, Peru, Japan, and Africa. Grandma always brought her a souvenir from these distant lands, and Mom still had them in a box. She let me keep one of my favorites from Africa. It was a plump seed that was hollowed out. Five tiny elephants were carved from light wood, and they fit inside the seed. I'd look at them under my magnifying glass and try to figure out how anyone could carve details into such a speck of a thing. They were perfect elephants. I always wished that I knew who made it and what they were thinking about at that very moment. What was their name? And could they have any idea that a girl in North America was still appreciating their hard work, nestling the amazing seed in fabric to keep it safe?

Grandma also liked to tell me about the places she had seen, describing the people and their different customs. She said that I would enjoy traveling to other countries when I grew up. I have a cool photograph of her riding on a donkey up a steep, white path in Greece. She looked bursting with happiness. I'm so glad she was able to have her dream of traveling come true.

She now lived on her own, and she drove back and forth to her volunteer activities at a hospital, a high school, and Meals On Wheels, where she delivered packaged meals to home bound seniors. She was usually older than the people she served. She had many award certificates for all the hours that she worked helping others. I hoped she would live until she was way over a hundred.

I really only had my mom and Grandma Reilly to talk to about anything, since Noah spent a lot of the year with his dad. I didn't feel lonely, but I wished that I was in a big family with permanent brothers and sisters. Grandma said she understood, because she used to wish that, too.

I wondered if my mom sometimes felt bad that we were on our own. She didn't want me to know that she worried about money and having enough to survive. But when she was doing the bills, she often leaned her head on both hands and just stared at all the papers and envelopes.

After our divorce, we had moved south from Orlando to a place called Saint Cloud, because Mom wanted to live in a small town. I like the name of it, as if it was built high up in the sky. Saint Cloud is next to an enormous lake with a long Indian name that means "we will gather together here." There are many places in Florida that have Native American Indian names. It doesn't seem right to me that settlers took the land away from the people who lived here, even killing a lot of them. They were people who knew how to live in harmony with nature and each other, so they probably would have shared.

We would occasionally see alligators swimming near the shore of the lake when we went on nature walks. The alligators always seemed like they were waiting to pounce on something, floating along like a prehistoric dream, leathery heads drifting across the dark surface. I had heard about a kid that got pulled in by an alligator down by the beach, but my mom said the older kids were just trying to scare me. I didn't understand why they had wanted to scare me, because they didn't even know me. Alligators never mess around when they want something. They'll grab it and lock down with their jaws, yanking it under-water and spinning in circles until it drowns. They don't really like to eat people, because I think we're too big for them to swallow. They prefer fish.

I could only go on nature walks when my mom was with me, since we never knew where the alligators might be. We usually stayed on the sidewalk near the lake, unless there was garbage to clean up closer to the water, then I held the bag while Mom picked up the food wrappers, cups, and other items that we found. She said we needed to help take care of our world. It was a bit frustrating to see trash on the ground when there were garbage cans all along the sidewalk.

My mom worked as a pediatric home care nurse, taking care of disabled children. None of them could breathe on their own or get out of bed by themselves. I'd met a couple of them when she took me with her to go in for an emergency. She was good at getting them to smile and laugh. I was always extremely grateful to be able to walk and breathe on my own after visiting with them, and I wished that their doctors could cure them, so that they would be able to walk around, too. Mom sometimes worked extra hours on the weekend to make enough money for us, but it made me glad to know that she was helping people, even though I wanted to spend more time with her. I was still trying to find a way to convince her that I could stay home alone.

I didn't watch TV often, but I enjoyed documentaries about animals and science and some of the history stuff. My mom never watched much TV either, but we both liked a good movie. Channel twenty-four was the public station, which was better because they didn't ram commercials down your throat every eight minutes.

Mom said that I absolutely couldn't watch any of the afternoon reality shows, but I had seen those shows at Ashley's house, the people arguing with each other and talking about how terrible so and so treated them and who was right. There were even ladies who would fist fight over men, and some of the things they fought about had to do with sex. That kind of talk made me really uncomfortable. Nobody needed to say those things on TV for everyone to hear.

Mom told me that the people who made those shows likely believed they would receive more money by including violence and sex, because they thought more people would watch. She said programs sometimes caused people to mimic the behavior of what was shown to them, because people learn by example, especially children. I realized that programs can program people.

If you watched those shows every day, you might believe that the whole world was angry and sad, full of people looking for ways to blame each other for their problems and waiting to attack one another. So, people chose to argue and fight, and then countries ended up arguing and fighting. If someone looked at us from another planet, they might think we were angry savages.

I liked when a show had a story about a miracle, because it left you feeling happy after you watched it. There could be programs that only showed miracles, and then you would keep smiling about it for the rest of the day and be programmed to expect them. My mom said that miracles were likely always happening, we just didn't get to hear about them very often.

I wanted Mom to see a miracle soon, because she was still quite sad. She usually went into her room to talk to Karin on the phone at night, and she had a tired look around her eyes. I knew that the accident had changed her way of being. She became extra protective of me, keeping me closer to her, and telling me to pay attention whenever we walked through a parking lot.

One night, I heard her talking to Karin about the dream she'd had back when Karin was pregnant with Brody. Fay and Karin had flown from Arizona to visit us while she was pregnant. Mom's dream occurred a few weeks after they left. She had woken up in a sweaty panic, shouting and crying. She called Karin that afternoon when she was calm enough to ask her to be careful around cars, that she'd had a dream that Karin and her baby were in a car accident.

She explained to me that people can experience déjà vu, as if they had already seen an occurrence, and how people can have dreams that sometimes give glimpses of the future. She called it intuition, and said that everyone has intuition, which doesn't come from thinking, but from a sudden burst of knowing.

Mom told me that she didn't want to say such a thing to Karin back then, but felt she had to warn her since the dream was one of her dreams that stood out. She'd had other dreams like that one that people had known about which had also come true. Karin knew about her dreams, so she had promised that she would be extra careful around cars.

On the phone that night, Mom was telling Karin that it wasn't Karin's fault, that she was an excellent mother who had done everything possible to keep him safe, and that toddlers moved quickly. Mom reminded her that she'd had to jump in and lift me up from the deep end of a pool when I had fallen in, and that another time when I was a toddler, I was found in the middle of a highway after I had quietly roamed out of the house. I wished Karin wouldn't blame herself for the accident. It would be good if we lived closer to them so we could help out, and then I might even be able to stay with them while Mom worked.

In our apartment building a retired teacher lived down the hall from us, and she was home all day while her husband worked. We didn't know her very well, but she offered to watch me during the summer. Mom had decided that she didn't want me to be at Ashley's house, because she knew that they kind of ran loose, like watching those reality shows in front of me and bringing me with them when they went on errands. So, it looked like I might have that lady, Mrs. Miller, taking care of me.

Mom and I tried to find a book about how to feel better after you lose a child, but Karin ended up telling her not to buy one because a lot of people had given her books like that. She said that it was too hard to concentrate for very long on anything. She had frequent nightmares about the accident, which always woke her up screaming. She was still trying to save Brody night after night.

A friend of theirs officially named a star after Brody and sent them a big map of nearby constellations, so they would know exactly where to look in the sky to see Brody's star. I wished that I knew where it was, and then I could look up and see it shining. There was no way to count all the stars in the universe, so they would definitely need a map to find it. I wondered how much it cost to buy a star. I wanted to buy them a time machine to go back and change everything.

# CHAPTER 5

∞

I COULDN'T WAIT to start fourth grade, not that I
didn't like sleeping in and doing my own thing during
the summer. The problem was that Mrs. Miller was
in charge of me whenever my mom was at work.
Mom paid her to stay with me in our apartment. She
believed that I would be safer at home, so Ashley's
house was no longer an option, even to go over and
visit. Mrs. Miller wasn't mean—well, maybe rather
stern, but she hummed all the time. She also liked to
talk on our phone, so I couldn't go on the Internet
very often because we had a dial-up connection. And
then there was part of the day when she wanted to
be in her apartment to get cleaning done or dinner
started for her husband. I would bring a book, even
though she usually talked me into helping her clean.

Grandma said that the summer would be over
before I knew it. I was still waiting for her to tell me
about life and God. She had sent me new articles to
read, really good ones. They were about scientific
information, like the one that explained how electrons

move around inside atoms, and how the human body is made of atoms, the very same thing everything else is made of when you get right down to it.

There was another article about studies that were done to learn the effects of our thoughts on our bodies. They hooked people up to equipment that monitored their brain waves when videos were shown to them, and then they tested their blood to learn about the chemicals and hormones that are produced by emotional reactions. There are millions of things called peptides that are released when we think, and different types of peptides go zooming into the cells of our bodies whenever we feel an emotion. Then the peptides change how our cells function due to how we feel. Emotions can actually change how our bodies work. This seemed important enough to be taught in school, but I had never heard about it before.

I still thought about Brody, a lot. He had just started to talk, but he never had the chance to live long. Fay was an only child now. We could have moved to Phoenix to live by Karin, but my mom said she would never live in that city again. I don't think she had a very good time back when she lived there.

I wished that I was old enough to get a job. I tried to think of ways to make money, but Mom wouldn't let me go off on my own to clean apartments or walk dogs. I didn't like to see her working so hard, and I wanted to be with her more often. When I'm old enough, I can get a real job, and then I'll buy her air conditioning for her car and lots of dark chocolate.

I finished another article that Grandma emailed to me, and my mind was trying to take in all the details. I poured myself a glass of water and sat down at the kitchen table. There were children who had died from an accident or an illness, and then they had suddenly come back to life. While their bodies remained still, they had a glimpse of life after death. I was amazed. It was a place that you never wanted to come back from. Not even to be with their mothers did these children want to return. They were disappointed to be back in their bodies. This information helped me the most, because it meant that Brody still existed! He was safe, and he was enjoying life in a grand way.

The phone began to ring, so I ran and grabbed it.

"Well, darling Rylee! How are you this fine day?"

"Oh, Grandma! I'm glad you called! I just read about heaven and the children, and I'm so happy about it! There are colors we've never seen before and awesome music, and you feel full of love every second. Can you imagine? And you get to be with family and still have parties!" I paused for a breath.

"Slow down there a minute, sweetie pie!" Grandma was laughing.

But I was on a roll. "So that means we'll always get to be together, for real! Those kids didn't want to come back, not even the youngest ones who should have wanted their moms. They said that they were *way* happier than they had ever been. Nothing was bad or sad or scary. They could even see their bodies as they were leaving, and it didn't bother them. This is so good to know!"

"I had a feeling you might enjoy reading about it," she said. "There are many articles and books about near death experiences. Some of them were written by doctors who studied it for years and interviewed hundreds of adults and children. They found remarkable similarities in their accounts. It's fascinating information."

"So you've read some of the books?"

"Yes, I have. Another thing that's interesting is that many of the people who came back from heaven had different religious beliefs, and some of them didn't even believe in God."

"Really? That's great!" I felt a growing sense of relief for the whole world. This meant that people from different religions were together in heaven, and that heaven was for everyone! Like the very best ice cream party, all flavors were included. I wondered why some people wanted to believe that only their group would get in.

"Grandma, it would be a lot more fun to invite everyone to the party."

"You're something else, my girl." She sounded amused. "Have you ever heard the expression, 'When the student is ready, the teacher will appear'?"

"I don't think so."

"What do you suppose it might mean?" she asked.

I liked that she always gave me a chance to figure things out. "Maybe it means when you're ready to know something, the right person comes along to teach you."

"Exactly," she confirmed.

"So, *you're* my teacher! And I'm the student. I'll bet you're going to tell me about God now, huh?" I had been waiting for a long time, and I realized that I wasn't as angry about the accident. I was still sad, but anger had made me feel stuck in a hard place, so it probably wouldn't have been the right time to learn about God.

"Rylee, I'd like to call you back in an hour, and then we can begin. Will you be available?"

"Um…sure," I answered slowly. I had to wait an hour!

"Think about this in the meantime. You can make your own decision about God. I'm going to share what I believe, after years of studying, seeking, and praying. But you can find out what rings true and pure to you. Make your own decisions about all that you consider. As time goes by, you may even expand on what you believe as life reveals a new insight.

"And you don't need to try to convince anyone that you're right and they're wrong. Your way of being is evidence of your belief. Everyone is different, because we're supposed to be. Would there be so many different types of people born if we're all supposed to be just the same? It may take some people more time to comprehend anything beyond the physical; necessary life experience might be needed for them to become receptive to spiritual information.

"So please don't judge anyone on their individual path, or they will not experience your kindness. The smallest favor or grace shared with another, even a smile, may be a turning point in their life. And I want to share this information with you, because I love you. I certainly could have used this understanding when I was your age."

I didn't want to wait an hour, but I needed to be patient.

"Rylee, are you still there?"

"Oh! Yes, I'm here. Sorry. I was listening."

"Will you think about what I just said?"

"Yes, I will. And I'll be waiting for you to call me, Grandma." I forced myself not to beg to hear it.

She replied, "Until then, the pleasure was most assuredly mine."

I giggled as we said good-bye. She made me laugh more than any kid I had ever known.

# CHAPTER 6

∞

I WAS EXCITED to hear what Grandma was going to tell me, and I believed that it was important. Our phone had a speaker button, so I set up my cassette tape recorder because I didn't want to forget anything she was about to say.

"Mom, Grandma's going to be calling me back soon," I announced. My mom was sitting at our desk in the living room. I walked up behind her to see that she was looking at a college catalog and writing down numbers. She had recently been talking about wanting to take classes to become a Registered Nurse as soon as we could save the money for it.

"Okay, Rylee. Hey, check this out. Here's a school that allows LPNs to do home study for their degree. Then there's only a long weekend for the clinical evaluation. I could still work *and* finish school. When we have a little more money, I'm going to go for it."

I glanced at the page of the catalog. "Looks good, Mom." I patted her shoulder and considered telling her about what Grandma was going to share with me.

"You've got your mind on something else, huh? Always thinking, my love. I know that Grandma is going to talk to you about God."

I was surprised that she knew, but then it wasn't the first time she knew what was happening with me. "Did she tell you?"

"She did. She asked for my permission to talk to you about it. Listen carefully to her, maybe you can explain it to me later." She laughed and reached out to hug me.

"All right, I will." I stopped myself from asking her more about it, because I figured she wouldn't tell me anyway.

"I'll be in my room," I said, picking up Mittens and carrying her down the hallway. Mittens had long gray fur that floated like silk in the air.

The phone rang an hour later. I turned the tape recorder on and answered the call.

"Well, I'm sure you've been waiting patiently," Grandma began. I could hear the smile in her voice. "Please remember that being patient will always help you enjoy life and not miss the good stuff while you're frustrated over something that's beyond your control."

"I'm working on it, Grandma." I was trying to sit close enough to be heard on the speaker phone. I waited quietly while she cleared her throat.

"That's fine, Rylee. Now, let's begin. For a few weeks, I'd like you to investigate your mind. I'll ask you to consider the way that you think. You can report back to me on the weekends to give me updates, and then we'll talk about everything you're learning. We can start our mission right away."

This was intriguing, but it didn't seem to be about God.

"For this first week, I'd like you to notice your thoughts and how you feel about what is on your mind."

"I'm not sure I understand what you mean."

"All right, please do this for a moment. Don't say anything. Just relax and try to keep track of your thoughts until I say stop. Okay?"

"Okay," I agreed. "Now?"

"Yes, begin right now."

I took a full breath, wondering where she was going with it, but I would just follow along. I really wanted to know about God.

I imagined Grandma pouring tea for me, like she did the last time we were there. I loved the tiny sugar spoon. It looked like a toy. I thought I heard Mom in the kitchen and wondered if it would be dinner time soon, and what we might have to eat. My stomach was feeling empty. Maybe we'd have grilled cheese sandwiches again. I hoped we still had potato chips left. Mom wanted to go back to school, but extra money had been scarce for a long time. Mrs. Miller was coming over in the morning for another day of humming. I wondered how little time I'd have on the computer because she'd probably be on the phone most of the day. Sometimes she even made me get off the Internet so she could talk to her friends, which was *very* rude.

"Stop," Grandma said. "Now, consider the subjects you were thinking about and what emotions went along with them. That was only twenty seconds."

"Really? I had a lot of thoughts in twenty seconds."

"What type of feeling did each thought create as it entered your mind?" she asked. "Did you notice that a feeling was attached to every thought?"

Hmm. I'd gone from a pleasant feeling when I imagined Grandma pouring tea, to feeling hungry, to wondering how much food was left, to being a little anxious about my mom's desire to be in school and our lack of money, to being frustrated about Mrs. Miller coming over, and then to being angry about potentially not having enough computer time.

"Grandma, that's wild. It was only twenty seconds? I had a bunch of different feelings about all kinds of things."

"You will do this your entire waking life. Brains prefer to remain active. But the important thing to notice is how you felt."

"I had a mixture of feelings, and the last ones were getting worse." Just mentioning this reminded me of how much I was dreading the upcoming day with Mrs. Miller, and I felt frustrated all over again.

"So you noticed that each thought had an emotion attached to it?"

I sighed heavily. "Yeah, I noticed that for sure."

"This is what I'd like you to do for the week," she suggested. "As often as possible, I'd like you to continue noticing and evaluating your thoughts, remaining aware of the different emotions that go along with them. How easily does one type of thought lead to another that's similar? What happens when you start thinking about something that bothers you? And then listen to people, see if you can tell what their thoughts are focused on by what they're talking about."

"Okay, I think I can do it." This seemed like a neat experiment. Maybe I could find an empty notebook and start a new journal.

"Now you have an assignment for lesson one. If you're able to do this for a week, you will always know how to keep tabs on your thoughts."

"I'll do my best," I told her. Even though it didn't appear to have anything to do with God, I figured that she would tell me more as we went along.

She was laughing. "I know you're wondering about this, Rylee. Just trust that it's a process you can learn step-by-step. This is all about connecting with God. Once you understand the process, you will realize how very simple it is."

"All right. I'm ready to learn! I'm going to keep a journal so I don't miss anything. I think you should also know that I'm recording you. I read somewhere that you're supposed to ask a person if you want to record a conversation."

"My dear, I think that's true if you plan on using this against me in a court of law." This really cracked her up. I loved her laugh.

"I promise to keep it away from *that* court," I replied.

We both laughed, and then I could tell that we were finished with the important talk.

"School begins soon. I can't wait! I hope my teachers are kind."

"A new season is here," she said. "Are you still doing your words?"

"Yes, I am. Mom's letting me choose them during the summer, so that's been fun." I got to pick the five new words from the dictionary to learn and try to use each week, rather than my mom picking them, like she usually did.

"Lovely," Grandma concluded. There was the creak of her rocking chair, so I knew she was getting ready to hang up the phone. She had never changed to a cordless phone, since her old one worked just fine.

"You're on the way, Rylee. And I love you enormously."

"I love you too, Grandma! It has been quite a supreme pleasure visiting with you today." I was getting fancy.

"Oh, but this supreme pleasure was positively all mine!"

We laughed together again. I turned the tape recorder off after we hung up because I wanted to have her laughter on tape. You never know when you might want to listen to a little piece of heaven.

# CHAPTER 7

—— ∞ ——

BOY, DID I ever think a lot. It was a challenge to keep track of all that crossed my mind. I should have asked Grandma if she wanted me to pay the most attention to what I was thinking or how I was feeling. At first, I tried to write down all the subjects that I rolled through each hour, but I would need many notebooks at that rate. So what I tried next was to stop thinking for part of the hour. Quieting the mind, this was tricky. It was like trying to shove the opposing ends of two magnets together, so close, and yet so far. Other thoughts would try to push their way in during the quiet, although I got better at it the more I tried.

I recognized a pattern as the week went by. If I was having a pleasant thought, other smooth thoughts followed that first thought easily, and I was happy. If I was feeling irritated by things happening around me—Mrs. Miller's humming being extra loud—I often had grumpy thoughts, which led me into grumpier thoughts, and then on to worried thoughts. Then I felt nervous and sad.

I also noticed what Mrs. Miller preferred to talk about while she was on our phone. She had one friend who seemed to really bring out her competitive side. They would compete to see who had the worst story about someone else or the most mournful tale about why their life was difficult. Even when she was off the phone, I could tell that she was still upset. She would often sigh and say things like: "I guess I'd better go start dinner for Joe, or else he'll give me grief about another measly sandwich." I could feel her bad mood lingering and lingering.

I realized that my mom hadn't been as cheerful since Brody's accident, but that was understandable. She didn't joke around as much, and she was quieter than usual. Plus, she was working long hours to save money for school. I knew it was going to take time. Grandma said that because Mom and Karin were so close, Mom was grieving along with her.

When I thought about anything related to the accident, a wave of sadness would wash over me. To stop the sadness, I remembered what Grandma had suggested, so I'd picture Fay laughing and playing, her cute dimples showing as she smiled. And I imagined Karin and John feeling extra comfortable and peaceful as they rested at night.

I called Grandma on Sunday afternoon. My notebook was open and my pen was uncapped, because I had decided to take notes while we talked. The tape recorder was ready for action, and I was feeling very efficient.

We got right down to business after our greeting. "This week was a long one, Grandma. I had no idea how busy a mind can be."

"I'm sure you kept close track of everything. You're a regular Dick Tracy."

Sometimes she lost me. "What?"

"Never mind, darling. Your ole Grandma can forget that you haven't been here that long. Now, tell me how it went."

"Okay. It was difficult to write down every thought. You know how your mind can go all over the place. So I wrote things down by main subject and strongest feeling. I noticed that whenever I thought of something that made me feel good, it was easy to continue thinking of other pleasant things. Of course, I felt fine then. But if something upset me, or if I thought of anything that made me worried, other negative thoughts started coming."

"Were you able to stop the negative thoughts?"

"I figured out a way to do it, although it wasn't easy at first. My thoughts would just speed right along unless I was paying attention to how I felt. But later in the week when I knew what was going to happen next, when I felt a sticky thought beginning, I made myself change to another subject. One that made me feel better."

"Nice!" she replied. "You're quite a natural."

"It just made sense. I sure didn't feel like keeping those heavy thoughts and itchy feelings. It worked well when I chose a better thought."

"That's wonderful, Rylee! You've just moved right into lesson two, which is all about how to feel peaceful and positive. Another terrific way to distract yourself from negative thoughts is to look around, no matter where you are, breathe deeply, and then find something to appreciate: the shape of a tree, the soft blue of the sky, a beautiful song you remember, how helpful an escalator can be, anything. This will allow you to break away from any negativity that was brewing. It's also called 'giving thanks,' but you don't have to be down on your knees to do it.

"Appreciating anything is being thankful. When you remain in a state of appreciation, you'll start noticing many things to appreciate. You are creating a peaceful set-point, no matter what is happening around you. This will become your point of attraction, this grateful state of being. You will open the door to a higher flow. Gratitude is a powerful energy. Let it flow. It's one of the quickest ways to bring more great things your way."

"I like that, Grandma."

"Me, too," she said. "But it may be challenging at times to find a better thought, like if you're feeling very sad. The remedy is to find a thought that's just a little bit better, even a grumpy thought. Those are better thoughts than extremely sad thoughts, only because you're gaining a little more control over how you're feeling, and then you don't feel as weak and hopeless.

"If you can then make the necessary climb from anger to frustration, you will be able to reach a lighter feeling place each time you choose a different thought. Once you get to frustration you can move up to disappointment, and then you'll be even closer to feeling hopeful again. Just keep going. You can't always jump right up to a wonderful feeling place from a terrible feeling place. But you can always climb the ladder one rung at a time to a higher place, using your thoughts and intentions. As you practice and become more aware, you'll find that it just keeps getting easier. Asking God to assist you is beneficial as you move along upward. It would be helpful to claim out loud, 'May I know myself in peace. I am in peace. I am knowing peace.' Now that you're learning how to maintain your mindset, you'll never want to forget. It's the important second step to connecting with God."

"I don't ever want to forget," I told her. "It works really well. I feel much better about everything."

"You will find that you become more skilled at it with daily practice. You're actually training your brain to develop new pathways. If you're ever faced with a big problem, even one that feels huge, you must not remain focused on the negative. You may work it around in your mind a bit, but if you can't find a productive thought about the subject, leave it. Use the distraction technique to find the best feeling thought that you can, about anything, even if it's only a tiny bit better. Because that better thought will be followed more easily by an even better one. You will make progress away from the negativity. If you get thrown off once in a while, not to worry. You know what to do, so just take charge again. No one and nothing else controls your mind but you. You choose how you want to feel in every single moment."

"I really like that! I didn't know I had so much control over the way things seem to make me feel. Nothing can *make* me feel a certain way unless I let it. I'm the one choosing my thoughts. I get it!"

"You've got it! Now, did you notice other people and their thinking habits?"

"I did. I noticed that Mrs. Miller does a lot of negative thinking. It seems like she tries to find something that upsets her just to tell her friends about it. Almost like she enjoys it." I thought of Mrs. Miller's face and the thick lines between her eyebrows. She always seemed to be frowning.

"People can develop habits of thinking and feeling, often from childhood, which they sometimes can't break free of as easily because those familiar pathways have been used for a long time. They may not know how to leave the old patterns of thinking behind. And when they start the bitter thinking, more negative thoughts follow right along, until they're nearly drowning in them. Then they look around and see how bad everything seems to be, and they call it proof that they were right in the first place.

"This can create an odd kind of satisfaction, this apparent confirmation of the desire to be right, even about something negative. So there they will often stay. People can also get used to the habit of harsh thinking because it's a familiar way of operating. There can be a form of comfort found in anything familiar, even if it is not beneficial.

"And life can be challenging when people frequently blame themselves. Guilt is like a bee sting, very painful when it first occurs, and then it causes a deep ache. It is also necessary to remove the stinger of guilt before it infects the body.

"We can always learn from our mistakes, and then make different choices. Everyone has the right to do this. No need to keep holding on to guilt. You see, it's very important to know that you are worthy of being and worthy of love, no matter what you have *ever* done or thought. You are always worthy of love."

"I'm glad about that!" I laughed.

"Yes, indeed. It's often beneficial to talk to someone, to reach out for help. But a problem can become more solidified if people continually share their sorrows. Then they keep the negativity alive, and it can grow into a heavier burden. When you speak about anything, it adds weight to the intention. You remind yourself of how bad you're feeling, and reinforce the idea of just how bad things seem to be, when you continue to think about it and tell others.

"Life can present challenge and there may be discomfort or loss to rise up from, but you don't have to recreate your past by frequently focusing on it, dragging it right along with you. You can make a fresh choice in each and every moment."

"This is good news," I say to her.

"It's wonderful news. And you are a natural, my dear. All children are naturals."

"I want to hear another lesson, Grandma. Do I have to wait?"

"No, you don't have to wait. Let's move right along."

# Chapter 8

$\infty$

"Lesson three will come easily to you, because you have a keen imagination. Do you like to daydream?" she asked.

"Oh, yeah. My teacher used to catch me doing it in math class. I never meant to drift off, and then the next thing I knew, she was calling on me."

"Well, drift away, my girl! Although maybe not in math class, if you want a good grade. Here is the third lesson: You get what you expect."

The words didn't go in all the way. "You get what you expect? Grandma, are you trying to be elusive?" This was one of my vocabulary words for the week, which I'd been waiting to spring on someone.

"Heavens, no. Not me. Rylee, would you please hold on a moment while I pour some more water?"

"Sure." I was thinking about the new lesson. It sounded good, but it still didn't sink in very far.

"All right, I'm back now," she said. "Have you ever heard about athletes using something called visualization?"

"No, I haven't."

"Visualization is daydreaming with a purpose. When athletes want to perform in an optimal way, they often do it by thinking ahead. They take time imagining themselves going through the motions of their event in a fine manner. They go over it, visualizing it in their mind's eye, seeing and feeling the achievement of it before it even occurs. They remain positive about it, not worrying that they will fail. Then when they finally perform, they're usually successful.

"A vivid imagination is a powerful tool. You may get what you are focused on. You may get what you expect. Label it any way you'd like, the result is the same. The reason is because every thought is actually a 'prayer' in the sense that it is received by God."

"Gosh, every thought?"

"Not to judge you, Rylee. Just in awareness of your expectations."

I was eager for a full explanation. "So how can I get what I expect?"

"By understanding that your thoughts are being received by the Source of all things. And knowing that what you think often determines what you will get. What you think, what you believe, is what you are matched up with, and you may then experience situations that match your expectations. When you think about something in a consistent way and believe that it might be, whether or not you want it to actually occur, it may take place because you are attracting it.

Or something might happen that is similar to what you believe could be. It usually doesn't happen right away, which is why most people haven't recognized the process.

"Many people spend a lot of time worrying. All the visualization that goes on in this case is done in a negative way. They spend time worrying about the possible ways that something could happen, dreading the idea of living it out, wondering what their friends would think, and gathering stories about others it has already happened to, even though they still hope that it won't occur. Their consistent focus and strong emotion on the subject increases the likelihood that this type of situation may become a reality. Without meaning to do it, they're expecting the worst."

"But how can that be?" I asked. "I mean, what makes it happen that way just from their thinking about it?"

"Now hold on to your hat!" she announced. "The reason is because God matches us with what we expect, what we believe. You will most often receive what you expect. God left it up to us to choose for ourselves, which is called free will. Everyone has free will and a creative consciousness. Your consciousness is your awareness. Your awareness is creative. Everyone is getting what they expect. It's been this way for all of time. We just haven't fully connected with the way that it works."

"How does it work?"

"It works because of a principle based on magnetic force. The entire universe that God created relies on magnetic force to function every second. Even down to the tiniest of particles, the atom, where magnetic force keeps the electrons spinning in a harmonious manner. It keeps us physically alive. Every atom in each cell of our bodies must maintain this magnetic balance. And without the magnetic force of gravity, we would fly up into space, and the planets would not stay in orbit around the sun.

"We're utilizing magnetic force every day in loads of inventions: telephones, televisions, clocks, tape recorders, and many more. Magnetic force is constantly at work, keeping our bodies, our world, and the entire universe in balance.

"Our thoughts produce a strong energy signal, a magnetic request, that the field of God receives. We then experience situations that match what we requested. We magnetically attract what we expect, and it is reflected back to us in our daily lives. If someone believes that they will always be poor, they are expecting it. If they pray to God for help, but still hold the belief that they will likely never have what they require, they are still expecting to remain poor. They will get what they expect. Our free will allows us to choose. We attract, or get, what we expect. Do you still have the magnet set that I sent you for Christmas?"

"Yes, I love it," I say excitedly. "I was just thinking about magnetic force today!"

"Well, imagine that!" she laughed. "There is such power in the force that draws the two ends together. But can you see that force?"

"No. It even goes through stuff. Solid stuff like a table! When I put a magnet on top of the table and moved another one underneath, it looked like the top one was moving all by itself." I was looking forward to more experimenting.

"And when you try to stick the wrong ends together, it's impossible to do," she continued. "You feel that if you try hard enough, you can mash them together, but the magnets will never touch one another. Such energy in metal rods, and in the universe! But the magnets only go together one way, just as God cannot connect you with something other than what you have magnetically attracted by your expectation. It does not fit in with the plan that God has used, across the board, for our entire world and universe to function.

"You attract what you are truly expecting. Your expectation is the main signal that is being recognized by God. Your most frequent thoughts, your ideas, and the emotions that are created by them build your belief system. Your beliefs hold your real expectations.

"Your desires and spoken words are often changing moment to moment. But your belief system holds your real expectations, and those core beliefs are what you will attract, because you expect that they are so. And they may be so for you, if you continue holding on to them.

"Prayers are thoughts, and thoughts *are* prayers. God does not need ears to hear everyone, because our thoughts and emotions transmit the energy signal of our expectations every second. God will provide your true needs, but you must expect this, which means that you must believe it and be open to receive it, even if it happens differently than you thought it might. The Source of all things knows what you require for your highest growth more clearly than you do, and is ready to provide for you.

"You don't need to decide that things must happen in a specific way, because you could block something perfect that may arrive for you. If you remain open to unlimited potential, you will clear the deck for wonder, wonderful happenings for you.

"So you can know that your true needs are coming to you, because that's what believing really is—it's knowing. Knowing is also having faith. You get what you expect, so you can choose to believe that your needs will be met in the highest way for your growth. God wants you to experience your life in the most beneficial way, so you can expect that this will be so.

"God's system, the same one applied to the creation of everything in the universe, operates in this fair, consistent way. God loves us, God is love, and this is a perfect plan for everyone. We are so very cared for, and we get to choose. Are you still with me?"

"Yes! This makes more sense than anything I've ever heard." My mind was swimming through all the new information. "Okay, so what we believe is what we're expecting *and* requesting, which can be different than what we're hoping to receive. And if we get to choose through our expectations, then whatever happens to us usually happens because we're expecting something like it, right?"

"That's right. Being this accountable can be challenging for people to accept. It might seem easier to blame someone or something else for unwanted situations, even our own past. Then people often hope that a few prayers during the week might keep everything in balance, but the world is not yet a peaceful place. Most of all, people are not living in the fulfilling way that they could be living on a daily basis.

"We may not be able to reach the entire world right away, but we can certainly enjoy our lives, knowing how it all consistently operates in each and every moment. You get way more than three wishes, my dear."

"Oh, I love that, Grandma!" I felt goose bumps beginning, tingling in a nice way. "And I'm so glad that I have the tape recorder going."

"I hadn't planned on delving so far into it right now. It would be good for you to listen to your tape a few more times, because I want you to absorb it so it will stay with you. And I will simply know that this is going to sink in fully for you. I will imagine you completely understanding all of this, which is part of the system. You can help other people by holding supportive thoughts about them. Your thoughts can actually assist others."

"Wow! That would be great!" I thought of Karin and her family. Then I remembered Grandma's suggestion to imagine them finding peace and sleeping well. She had been slipping good ideas to me for a while.

"Have you told Mom about this? I know you asked her if it was all right to talk to me about God."

"Your mother has had extreme challenge in her life. Because of her early experiences, she believed that the world was full of danger. And since she is a powerful co-creator, just as we all are, her world was full of danger for a long time. It has taken her many years to leave the past behind and find stable ground. I've shared my beliefs a little at a time, knowing that she may need to hear it slowly. If I had presented it to her all at once, she might have become closed off because others have attempted to control her. This tragedy with Karin's family, she is still feeling it; her friend is suffering."

"Poor Mom!" I exclaimed. I wanted to help her. She needed to know how it worked so she could feel better.

"Rylee, I understand that you're concerned for her, but you can choose to resist thoughts that promote a negative reality. Let your sympathy be in the form of support rather than worry. Worrying about her will match you up with more things that may worry you, just as being frustrated or angry at someone and thinking bad things about them may bring you more things that could frustrate or anger you.

Angry thoughts can attract more situations that could bring out your anger, and worried thoughts can bring you more to worry about.

"So instead of 'poor Mom' think, 'I sure love Mom!' or 'Mom is feeling just fine.' Then use your imagination to hold images of your beautiful mother at peace. Believe it with all of your might, feeling the emotion now that you will feel as it comes true. You have the ability and power to help her, more than you could ever believe is possible. This leads me right into lesson three's experiment for next week. But first, let's gather up what you've learned so far."

"Okay," I replied, feeling humbled. I still had a lot of learning ahead. I didn't realize that I could have added to my mom's sadness by my worries for her, creating more worries for both of us. Yikes! I wanted to figure it all out. I listened intently as Grandma went over the lessons.

"Lesson one: Keep the direction of your thoughts flowing in a beneficial way. Your emotions are your reliable guide to doing this. Every thought creates an emotion within you. That emotion will let you know if the thought is worth continuing. Slow down enough to notice your feelings; it's well worth your time.

"Lesson two: Feeling peaceful is important. So if a thought feels harmful, stop it. Or if you must, think it through quickly, looking for lighter ways to reflect on the subject to resolve it; otherwise, change to a better feeling subject. Don't stay there, wallowing in worry, sorrow, anger, guilt, and fear any longer than necessary, because an avalanche of negative thoughts gains momentum and attracts more of the same. Climb up the ladder, no matter what. These thoughts are received by the field of God. The Source of all things matches you up with what you're attracting. You can request another delicious helping of bliss or another rough helping of misery."

"I'd like delicious things," I laughed.

"Don't we all, darling!"

"Now, lesson three: You get what you expect. God created a perfect system that functions throughout the entire universe, and this plan will allow you to rise to your highest potential. Each person gets to help co-create what they will experience and receive. You can believe that what you truly need is on its way, and then notice all the wonderful things around you in the meantime, appreciating God's perfect system in action every moment. Then leave the details up to God, because God ultimately knows your true needs. Something new may happen in a way that surprises you, even something beyond what you could ever imagine. Just let go and let God."

"I've heard that one, Grandma! I just wasn't sure what it meant."

"Your eyes are going to be wide open now, Rylee. You will likely see evidence all around you that what I'm saying is true."

"This is exciting! And it sure explains a lot."

"Yes, it certainly does. I must be going in a few moments. I need to go over and pick up the food for everyone. Those meals won't have wheels if I don't get moving! So, here is what…oh, please excuse me," she said, starting to cough. I heard her clearing her throat and taking a drink.

"Let me guess," I offered. "I'm going to see how I can help myself and others by the way that I think, imagining and expecting that all is well."

"Splendid! I couldn't have said it any better. You're going to teach many people in your lifetime. People will feel your loving energy."

"The first person I want to help is Mom, so then she can help Karin. And then Karin can help Fay and John. Hey, it just keeps going!"

"As I mentioned, you're going to teach many people. I love you dearly, and it has been a great pleasure."

I hadn't felt it so fully before. "The pleasure has been all mine, Grandma. I love you so much."

# CHAPTER 9

∞

WHEN I WALKED out of my bedroom, Mrs. Miller was already on our phone. I'd slept so deeply that I couldn't even remember if my mom came in like she usually did to kiss me good-bye. I felt a little grumpy seeing Mrs. Miller stretched out with her pale feet on our couch while she watched the morning news and jabbered away.

I cleared that thought from my mind by looking forward to a cold drink of apple juice. My stomach made a funny gurgling sound. I was so hungry that I decided to toast two waffles. While pouring the syrup, I began paying attention to what Mrs. Miller was talking about.

"I know it's just a depression. But it could easily turn into a tropical storm and then a hurricane," she said, trying to convince her friend. "Yep, it's coming this way. We need to keep a close eye on it. Uh-huh, don't you know it! We may be in for the big one."

I didn't want to hear about hurricanes so early in the morning. It was not a good way to start the day. Those monster storms, the thought of them scared me. August was the month when the hurricane season picked up, so I would just have to get used to hearing about them until November when the season ended. I sifted through the facts to reassure myself. Central Florida had been safe from the eye of a hurricane for decades; we were in the middle of the peninsula, protected by fifty miles of land. The odds were in our favor. I felt much better after reassuring myself.

The mixture of butter and maple syrup was perfect, and so were the lightly crisp edges of the waffles. It was easy to maintain a state of appreciation with food. While I ate, I read over a list of the supplies that I would need for fourth grade. I liked to read something while eating, even the ingredients on the side of a cereal box. My school list had items for Mr. Hamlin's class. He was known for his unusual science experiments and letting students use microscopes, so I was excited when I found out that he would be one of my teachers.

Mom and I still needed to go shopping for all of my supplies, including some new clothes. I had grown so much that my shoulders felt trapped inside my sleeves. I wore one of her T-shirts for a nightgown because I felt like a mummy in mine.

I spent most of the day in my room and on the patio with Mittens, listening for whenever Mrs. Miller hung up the phone so I could go online. Hurricanes were the big news of the day, and she needed to tell practically everybody in the phone book that one might be coming.

We had an unspoken agreement that we would let each other do our own thing. She never tried to play with me or do art projects, which was fine because her humming would've been too loud up close. That was the one good thing about her being on the phone— she never hummed. As much as I tried to expect a peaceful day with Mrs. Miller, the humming was not easy to feel good about. It seemed like it filled the whole apartment when she really got going.

She talked to me for a little while about school, and I was surprised that she actually seemed interested. Later, while she was reading a magazine, I tried to imagine her being silent, but that lady had different plans for her humming throat.

When my mom walked in the door after work, it felt like I had won a prize.

"How is my sweet girl doing today?" she asked as she reached out to me.

Mrs. Miller picked up her bag, said good-bye, and hurried down the hall and out of my daily existence. School started the next day!

"I'm doing pretty well, Mom. How was your day?"

"A good day for me, and especially for Nicholas. I think they may try to wean him off the ventilator soon. He's making such wonderful progress." It usually took her a while to come out of her nursing mode.

"Are you hungry?" she asked, looking in the refrigerator.

"Oh, yeah. It's been nothing but bread and water around here."

She turned to me with a smile, shaking her head. "Rylee, your long, grueling summer of Mrs. Miller watching you is already a thing of the past. The prisoner has been released. You may walk out this door in freedom." She motioned dramatically toward the door. "And I'll go with you, all the way to the restaurant and then on to the store."

I laughed with her. "Okay, Mom. Let's go." It was my end of summer outing, and we were both eager to leave.

There were few open tables in the busy restaurant, and I noticed that several people were discussing the tropical depression and talking about stocking up on supplies. We started to eat more quickly because we thought the store would be getting crowded. As we emptied our trays into the garbage and recycling bins, Mom said that someone could invent edible packaging so there wouldn't be as much going into landfills.

After we finished my school shopping, making our way around the crowded store, Mom wanted to pick up a few hurricane supplies. "We can always use these things later, you know," she said, trying to sound casual. But she ended up taking a lot of time looking at prices and putting most of the things back on the shelf. I was tired by the time it was our turn in the long checkout line, and I still needed to go home and organize my school supplies.

Thursday was an odd day to begin the school year, but I figured that it would give us a little taste of school and then let us have time over the weekend to adjust. I finished writing my name on everything. I tried to write in calligraphy on the front of my notebooks, but the smelly permanent marker didn't work for it. I had a calligraphy marker, but it dried up. It was my favorite one for writing poems. I finally arranged everything to fit inside my new backpack. My mom had let me buy a snazzy one with gel cushions inside the straps because she didn't want my shoulders to hurt from the weight of the books.

Going to sleep the night before the first day of school was never easy. There were so many possibilities ahead that I couldn't stop thinking about it. Wait a minute...I smiled. I could stop. I slowed my thoughts down as I turned over on my side. Then I imagined myself tired, like I always felt when I wanted to stay in bed on mornings when I had to get up. I began to feel relaxed and cozy. I would be dreaming soon. I was breathing slowly and deeply. It felt like I was sinking down into my soft pillow. My eyelids started to feel too heavy, and then I fell asleep.

In the morning, Mom dropped me off at school so I wouldn't have to start the child care program right away. I knew that I wasn't the only one who'd had a little trouble resting well. There were many sleepy-eyed kids, some looking around nervously for the right way to go. It was easy to spot the kindergartners each year. Many of them were trying not to cry as they stood close to their parents. I had sympathy for them, so I imagined them playing and happily meeting new friends, reporting to their parents at the end of the day that they'd had fun.

Mr. Hamlin was a lively teacher! I could tell that he loved teaching by the way he spoke, full of enthusiasm. He was kind, but I could also tell that he wouldn't let the rowdy kids get away with any shenanigans.

There were examples everywhere of the lessons that Grandma shared with me. A lady who worked as a lunch server the previous year was still working there. She was known to be mean, always telling us to hurry up, slapping the mashed potatoes down harder than necessary.

I watched her as I moved forward in the line, and I noticed that she seemed upset even when she wasn't rushing us along. Her thoughts might be about unpleasant things.

When she dumped a wet scoop of corn onto my tray, I told her, "Thank you *very* much."

She looked surprised and then suspicious, so I smiled at her. I looked into her narrowed eyes, believing that she could feel the relief of peace.

She just stared at me, but then one side of her mouth lifted into a smile, and she said, "Oh, you kids."

I'd never seen her smile before. She looked kind of cute. I felt a surge of happiness for both of us, as I continued smiling at her.

After I gave the cashier my ticket, I turned and saw the lunch lady glance my way. She nodded her head at me, and I knew for certain that people communicated with much more than words alone.

It was amazing what you could learn at school.

# CHAPTER 10

∞

THE TROPICAL DEPRESSION was the main topic on the news over the weekend. Mom usually didn't watch the news, because stations most often reported bad news. She told me that she would rather choose the news to learn about by reading it herself, but she turned on the TV when the local weather report began, just to check in.

I was still working on my project, trying to absorb all that I was learning. I had been listening to my tape and writing down what Grandma was teaching me, so my notebook was filling up quickly. I called Grandma in the afternoon, hoping she would be home. Florida was in a different time zone, so it was always one hour ahead of Iowa's time. I wondered if this meant that we were in the future.

"Rylee, what a nice surprise! It's so good to hear from you! I've certainly missed you." Grandma had a way of boosting someone up quickly.

"I've missed you, Grandma! It's been an exciting week."

"Life is such an adventure," she replied. "And how is school? Tell me about your marvelous new teachers."

"School is going to be fun this year! Mr. Hamlin already has an experiment planned where we'll get to look at different things under a microscope and try to figure out what's on each slide."

"Now that sounds right up your alley! It's incredible how everything is woven together. You'll get to find out just how perfectly formed it is when you look at it closely. The fabric of everything is divinely made. So, how did your other experiment go this week?"

I told her about the kindergartners and the lunch lady, and then I told her about Lisa, a new girl at school. At first it didn't seem like Lisa wanted to make any friends, but for some reason, I wanted to know her, so I imagined us being friends and laughing together. I smiled at her during recess, and then she walked over and asked if I wanted to swing with her. She was very funny after she got through being shy.

"I'm happy for you, sweetheart! There's nothing like a new friend to brighten your day."

"Grandma, what you've told me about is...like being able to fly. It didn't seem possible before. Now I feel better because nothing really bothers me too much anymore. I wish more people knew about this."

"Yes, Rylee. I do, too. You have to wonder why it's not more widely understood yet. Why don't more people know that their thoughts affect their reality? And imagine this, we're supposed to be able to do many more things, having been made in the likeness of God, the ultimate Creator."

"So if we were made in God's *likeness*, then we should be extra good at being able to create things," I said. "But, why don't more people know about this? I don't understand."

She hesitated before answering. "Well, I must tell you that I believe the true teachings were never fully revealed, because dictators didn't want people to recognize their own power. Leaders often used the strategy of fear to keep people in line, so their rules would be followed. Messages of freedom and fulfillment did not fit in well with such a goal, so the full teachings were hidden by those who were seeking to rule and command.

"And the potency of a powerful spiritual message can become obscured when groups of religious followers insist on proving their position. Many wars were started because of the desire to be right about spiritual beliefs. The message of love can be the focus, not the mission to show favored status.

"Individual peace is needed to achieve world peace, so one of the things that we're here to do is to help others experience a peaceful way of being. Because you're learning this while you're young, you won't encounter some of the obstacles that people can run into, such as being taught that they have little control over their lives, and that there's only one way that is right, so they must figure it out before they die, or else they might suffer forever in hell.

The do-or-die approach allows no room for true love and compassion. Oh, my dear girl, the world took a sharp turn and just kept on going," she concluded, sighing heavily.

I didn't like to hear any sadness in her voice, and I wanted to understand all that she was saying. I knew that I would have to listen to my recordings a few more times.

"Rylee, I wish to see love clearing the muddle that was created by greed and domination. But there will be a breakthrough. There will be an amplification of love, so we shall now move on!"

"Okay, great!" I said, feeling relieved. "I was wondering if there are more lessons."

"You will be pleased to find out that you will never stop learning. We get to learn and grow during every experience, making our way through all kinds of situations to the creation of new understanding. Your soul, the broader part of you, also learns and grows through your experiences here. You will *always* exist as an eternal being, so there really isn't a big rush to get it all done. There will always be more to experience in life, so take time to relish the ride. You will learn from each experience and then go forward with more knowledge of what to do differently on the next go-round.

"And you are forgiven, if you will also forgive others. This doesn't mean that you agree with what someone did. People can sometimes do harmful things, but you don't have to let it keep you in its grip. Without forgiveness, you can dwell in negative emotion, attracting even more of what you don't want. It's a vicious cycle. You're hurting yourself when you choose not to forgive. If you don't forgive others, you might remain in a place of judgment or anger, which may bring negative events into your life. And you must also forgive yourself, so you can move on without the ache of guilt.

"What you choose to focus on and believe will often be what is provided for you. To focus on the lack of anything that you require will likely keep it away from you. It can create more evidence of lack in your reality. And if you frequently complain, you could attract more situations to complain about. If you believe that the world is a dangerous place, it may appear that way for you. Whatever you focus on, you're inviting into your world.

"It is more beneficial to choose thoughts that allow you to feel eagerness, love, and appreciation. Get excited about something that you're looking forward to, even something basic like a snack or seeing a friend. When those powerful feelings begin, let your mind choose more wonderful thoughts, which will allow the fine feelings to grow and expand. Let those feelings flow through you for as long as possible. More situations will come along that provide a way for you to continue feeling eager, loving, and appreciative. If you get goose bumps, then you're likely beginning to feel the energy of the higher vibration."

"I do get goose bumps!" I laughed. "And I like how it feels. This is so cool!"

"Cool, indeed! When you're not chilly, those goose bumps often indicate that you're allowing Divine energy to flow through you. It's real energy," she said, happily. "Everything is energy."

I remembered the article I'd read about our bodies being made of atoms, and the spinning magnetic field within every atom. We were truly made of energy. And our thoughts were energy signals, magnetically attracting matching energy back to us. It was all coming together now.

"Wow! So we are actually energy." My mind imagined a computer screen that showed a strong energy wave peaking high and dropping low along with my thoughts. I really wanted to understand all of it.

"Grandma, are there any more lessons, like lessons one, two, and three?"

"There are three main lessons. Because you wish to learn, I'll share more. You have your tape recorder going, so I may as well continue in full. Let's row this boat all the way out!"

"Yes, please!"

"My eager girl," she replied, laughing gently. "Have you noticed how all of the lessons go together?"

I thought of the lessons again as I flipped through my notebook. "Hold on, please. I'm looking in my journal."

"Take your time, darling."

I found where I had written down a brief version of them.

Lesson one: Each thought creates an emotion within us that lets us know if it's a beneficial way of thinking.

Lesson two: Feeling peaceful is important, so if a thought feels harmful, stop it. God receives every thought like a prayer and matches you with what you're magnetically attracting. Distract yourself with another subject and notice wonderful things around you.

Lesson three: You get what you expect, so imagine living well, knowing that the Source of all things will provide your true needs. Believe it with all of your might, feeling the emotion now. Keep your faith strong and clear, without a doubt.

The lessons explained how to communicate with God. I suddenly had an image of Grandma working as an operator in front of a switchboard, plugging thick cables into a metal panel. She was someone who really knew how to make connections! Her job at the telephone company was teaching all of the operators how to make the connections correctly and efficiently, supervising the entire system of communication. This gave me those goose bumps again.

"You've been teaching me how to *actually* talk to God! It's all about the same thing."

"It certainly is! Each step in this communication process can be understood so you may make a full connection.

"And the system that God so lovingly created for us is available to *everyone* on the planet. No one is excluded from the power of God's perfectly designed system, just as nothing in the universe is excluded from the power of the magnetic force of gravity.

"Many people and groups of people have fought about the human idea of spiritual ownership. No one owns the rights to God's system—it just is. God is the energy of all existence. God is the fabric of all things. God is conscious awareness as pure love. Some people choose to join a group that claims to be the only one being cared for by God, as if God shouldn't take care of everyone else. If someone believes that they have the right to exist in a heavenly realm, yet they also believe that they are right to maintain the idea that others will perish and suffer, how is that of God? It is not. It is the very height of judgment. There is no love within that belief, only judgment that breeds conflict.

"The world moved so far away from the messages of peace and love that it became a war over rights. The earlier messages were given to show the way, the way to connect, not to transfer ownership of the system. People tend to stake their claim on things, but God's system does not have transferable rights.

"The field of God always responds to *everyone's* expectations, every moment, every day. And everyone is most assuredly invited to the party. Whether or not they accept the invitation to rise to the occasion is up to them.

"We can decide to accept our differences, as we each grow at an individual pace. Just as you need not punish yourself because of your past actions, so you must not judge another as they grow and develop. All the children in the sandbox must get along. It's time to drop the swords and recognize how close we have come to the brink of disaster.

"But we will not experience a final 'doomsday' scenario that ends our species, nor will we be over-taken by a group of dictators, because humanity at a higher level, a collective soul level, has chosen to realize the truth of our being, which is in unity with *all* of creation. We are finally moving beyond the idea of separation, the idea that God exists somewhere else, and that we are not one with Source, or with one another. We are now moving into unity. People will soon have a deeper awareness of themselves and of one another.

"Everyone and everything is connected. It has always been so, but humanity chose to learn through the belief in separation. This belief was only an idea that was agreed to and perpetuated throughout the generations. It was never true. Nothing can be outside of God, unless we attempt to place it there by the belief that it is outside of God. This is how all fear and the idea of lack were created. Humanity's choice to believe in the idea of separation created an opposite energy from the energy of love. It is this fear based 'anti-energy' that is now being reclaimed in truth, in the true vibration of everything, which is love.

"Humanity has done this on a massive scale, individually and collectively. Everyone is responsible for their creations, including a species. As we move beyond the idea of separation, we will be reclaiming all that was placed outside of God due to our witnessing it as such. The impact of our conscious attention is *far* more potent than we have recognized. The presence of the Divine has been denied and concealed by humanity's core belief that it does not exist, or that it exists elsewhere. This experience of separation is the world that has been created.

"It is time to claim love everywhere, in everyone, no matter how outside of God it appears, or someone chooses to appear, for that is where love is needed most."

"Wait a minute, Grandma. What about people in the world who do cruel things? How am I supposed to love them?"

"It doesn't mean that we agree with what someone is choosing to do, or that we need to give them a hug. Not at all. It is not even necessary to speak to them to do this. Instead, we are simply recognizing the truth of their being, which must be of God, because nothing can be outside of God. All is of Source, or nothing can exist. You are recognizing the Source of them, not how their personality is choosing to act. You just know that they are of love, of God, because it's actually impossible to not be of Source. But people may hold the belief that they are separate from God, or that God doesn't exist, which creates the experience of it. We get what we expect. We get what we believe.

"Your steady, loving perception informs them energetically, which helps to remind them of their connection, because they may have forgotten it. You are helping them to remember the truth of their being by recognizing them as of Divine love. This can also be done from far away, because words are not necessary for the energy to flow to them. Energy naturally rises when a higher vibration joins it. The more certainly you believe that the Divine is present, the more fully the presence of the Divine is revealed to you. This revelation is how the world is made new, as the rising tide of love flows higher.

"It may not be obvious now, but this great shift is well underway. The old systems of control are ending, and fresh new ways are being born that will benefit *everyone*. We are making history now; it is not making us. We have the ability and the right to choose a much higher way to exist. Imagine if many people realized this and began to claim everything in love, how quickly do you think the new systems would be born?"

"Oh, my gosh, Grandma! This is the best news, ever! It's going to happen fast, I just know it."

"That's the spirit, darling. *Nothing* can stop this shift. It's just a matter of how quickly humanity chooses to move forward into unity. Personalities can sometimes have their own agendas, as everyone moves forward at their own pace. Every single person makes a difference. And one loving individual may be the catalyst for the tipping point. A collective belief is most powerful.

"Imagine a peaceful future, then expect it. You are choosing a higher outcome for your children and grandchildren. We can choose to take care of one another, as we all take care of our Earth. Imagine this peaceful way to live and be loved. We *all* want to feel loved and appreciated, so just offer the same and it will come back to you a thousand fold.

"Once we unite in all of this new awareness, we will move forward rapidly to create a more peaceful planet. It is not only possible, it's right there, already set up and ready to go, only one thought away. And it would be so much fun!"

"Do you really think people would stop fighting if they knew about this?" I asked.

"Yes, because there would be no more fear of losing your freedom. We would all know that we're responsible for our own lives, that we do have a hand in choosing our experiences. Circumstances don't fall from out of the clear blue sky into our reality. We've usually requested them by our expectations—those constant prayers. There would be no more reason for blame, no more judgment and condemnation.

"We are all striving to exist and thrive, and we each have different challenges to meet. No one knows what someone else has come here to learn and experience. To stand in judgment of others may attract even more for you to judge harshly, and others who may judge you. The best way to live is to love everyone, no matter what. You then attract those who will love you, no matter what.

"And all of your creative power is in the present moment. Right now. There's no time like the present. The past is over, and the future never arrives, so remain present."

"You're right," I say, realizing that nothing else was happening, but what was happening right now. The past and the future were now just ideas. It is always right now. "Our minds sure like to go fishing around in the past, or trying to reel in the future."

She laughed. "Well put, Rylee! It's a pleasure to hear your unique ideas. And, you know, each of us is unique, but we are all from the same Source. Many different journeys will lead to a new awareness of God; some are short and straight, while others are long and winding. We can stay on our own path, being an example, and allow our brothers and sisters their chosen travels. Do not be a thorn on anyone's path. Plant the seed of love, and the elements will support the flowering of peace as it blooms. Even if a flower wilts, its sweet fragrance is still released into the world.

"This heightened understanding will lead to peace for families and countries and eventually the entire world. Maybe in your lifetime. There will be no more arguing about who should own the rights to God's love. We are *all* eternal beings, recognized by God, every single one of us. God's system of fulfillment is available to every human, without exception. What each of us chooses to do with our free will is simply up to us.

"The kingdom of God, the awareness of the Divine in all things, is truly within you, awaiting your agreement to it. Connect with it, and you will experience life beyond your wildest dreams."

"Grandma, you are very wise." I wanted her to run for president, but I wasn't sure if she would enjoy it, so I didn't say anything.

"And you are the sweetest girl I know. You asked for more, and I have just carried on, way up high on top of my soap box."

"But I like it! Please, go on. What you're telling me is really important." It felt as if a heavy door had swung wide open. The light came in, illuminating everything.

"Well, thank you for seeing me through, my dear. The rest of this is an expansion on the lessons. You may prevent disease by making this connection with God. Put the three lessons into action, and you will feel the balance in your body, mind, and spirit. Stay connected, and good health may be yours because you will not be stuck in fear, anger, guilt or sadness for any length of time.

"Do not focus on, or fear, an illness. No entertaining any thoughts of what you do not want. Just imagine your body being strong and healthy, no matter what. Even if you have symptoms of something, take control. Natural remedies and good medical care can assist you in healing, but the way that you think has an absolute effect on your body.

"And laughter really is good medicine, so have fun! It's important for your entire being. All the chemicals and hormones released when you smile and laugh strengthen your immune system more than any drug we could ever invent, not to mention how good it feels!

"And love yourself, as God loves you, unconditionally. Enjoy who you are without feeling the need to change your hair, your job, and your clothes before you will finally be satisfied. You're already so beautiful! You can feel content right where you are now, even if you desire something other. The Source of all things wants you to receive what you truly need, so don't block it by focusing on the absence of anything. It's very beneficial to feel appreciation and pleasure within your current state of existence. Grateful thoughts are powerful.

"There may be people who continue to step on their own feet, but for those people we can still send our supportive thoughts, continue living out our example, and wish them the best. Some people don't realize that they're choosing to feel bad, because they've never escaped the past, those habits of sour thinking about negative memories. Then they often dread, and continue to receive, more of the same. It requires new movement to break free from the past; one thought at a time *up* the ladder, as you leave the past where it belongs. When a person decides to rise, they'll quickly notice the fine results of this choice.

"You may also do your part by moderating your habits. You can't jump out of an airplane and expect to land softly just because you've imagined it as you're falling. Listen to your intuition—God is trying to tell you something.

"And love others, as you love yourself. When you give, in thought or deed, you actually receive. The well flows even higher for you when you share. To help another, even by focusing on a supportive thought for them, may also attract and bring you support, and it could come about right when you need it. The people you help may wish you well for your assistance, and then they might be more inclined to help someone else, and on and on."

"No wonder you're so healthy!" I say to her. "You have this stuff down!"

"Once you've experienced it, and you feel the pure connection, it's the only way to live. There's no going back. You can't let yourself, because you know how God's system operates."

I looked at what I had underlined in my note-book. "Grandma, you said that our core beliefs are what we're actually expecting, and that we usually end up getting what we expect."

"You are right on," she replied. "And this also applies to other people. What we expect from other people is usually what we get, or attract, from them. When we want someone to change, or to stop behaving a certain way, we often continue thinking about how much their behavior upsets us. If we continue to focus on the person's negative behavior, we can only attract what we're expecting from them. God's system applies to everything: to atoms, to our bodies, to nature, to gravity, to our journey around the sun each year, to God's constant awareness of what we're expecting.

"So, an effective way to help a person is to imagine them being well; visualize them healthy and strong, peaceful and content, whatever it is that might assist them. You're not trying to fix them to be the way that *you* want them to be. You're simply remaining positive in your own thoughts about them, allowing your focus on them, your witness, to lift them. We can help one another this way. Being angry at them only attracts more from them that may cause you to experience anger. Appreciate them, and they will likely show you more to appreciate."

"Now I understand why Mrs. Miller never stopped that humming. I was always thinking about how much it bothered me."

"It just follows along with the same principle, Rylee. Now imagine how it would be if you chose to witness everything in love, no matter what was happening around you. What do you think would come your way?"

"Hey, I want to try it! That would be a super way to live!"

I hesitated a moment, because I wasn't sure how the question that had been on my mind for some time could be answered, but I needed to ask. "I have a question. It's about Brody. I know you said that learning about God wouldn't explain why the accident happened. But Brody was just a baby. He couldn't have expected that."

"My love, many souls do not need a lot of time on Earth. In heaven there is no time. Brody probably enjoyed everything to the utmost while he was here. There is no true death, no final ending to existence. There is only a transition, a change. We will *always* continue to exist. And no one caused his death by worrying about him being hurt or dying. No one made it happen. If our thoughts could kill someone, people wouldn't need to use weapons in war, and I wouldn't want to drive in rush hour traffic.

"There is a rhyme and reason to the way that souls flow in and out of physical life. We will understand it later. They will be together again, and Brody knows this. It may be difficult for his family to live on without him physically here, until they understand that right now he's more fully alive and aware than he has ever been. He is part of the greatest love song ever imagined."

I remembered Mom saying that Brody was so focused on enjoying everything he did that even strangers noticed it. I thought of how he had studied my face while I played with him, his easy smile at everyone who looked his way. He was such an angel. "Maybe he wanted to come here to dance to the music for a little while."

"Maybe he did!" she replied. "Music is a wonderful way to experience joy, listening to it or making it. Music allows your spirit to soar and reach higher places.

"You see, many souls come here for only a short time. They come for important lessons and to bring their love here. Quality of life is not measured by quantity of years. Brody may have lived more fully than someone who has lived eighty years. Just know that all is well, my dear. God's energy never ceases being available to you, not even for one second. Now, do you have enough to think about for the week?"

She hadn't given me an experiment, but I didn't need one. "I definitely have enough to think about."

"I imagine that you're going to continue keeping a journal of your findings. Am I right?"

"You know me so well, Grandma."

"Rylee, I must say that it has been a divine pleasure visiting with you today. And I love you dearly."

"I love you too! But the pleasure has been all mine. Thank you so much!"

# CHAPTER 11

$$\infty$$

THE FIRST FULL week of school went well until I started hearing about hurricanes again. Charley had only been a tropical storm on Tuesday, but spun itself into a hurricane by Wednesday when it was near Jamaica. Tropical Storm Bonnie was also churning away out there, a day away from hitting another part of Florida. Mr. Hamlin had us doing a short unit on hurricanes. We learned about their formation off the coast of Africa and how hurricane hunters flew airplanes into the eye of a storm every few hours to get updated wind-speed readings and pressure measurements. They were very brave people.

I knew that I needed to get over my fear of hurricanes. My new friend Lisa had moved to Florida from Illinois, so she was nervous about being in a hurricane. She had seen a movie where people huddled together in their house during a hurricane. The entire roof had gotten ripped off in one piece, and the people went flying around. I wasn't the right person to help her feel better about hurricanes. There just didn't seem to be an easy way of thinking about them, and when I tried to change my thoughts to another subject, something would bring the topic my way again.

By Thursday afternoon, Central Florida was holding its breath to see where Hurricane Charley would be heading, because it had strengthened into a category two hurricane during the afternoon. This meant that its winds were between ninety-six and one hundred ten miles per hour.

At the end of class, Mr. Hamlin announced that there would be no school the following day. School was canceled throughout all of Central Florida. The next day was Friday the thirteenth, and some people were saying that Charley's arrival was going to be a disaster, just because it was the thirteenth. I realized how a superstition might come true if enough people believed in it.

Mom and I tuned in to hear the weather report at dinner time. Charley was now aiming for the Tampa area, which would keep the eye from directly crossing our county, but we were in for tropical storm force winds, tornado warnings, and flash flood watches because we would be on the more dangerous east side of it.

"Let's head out to the store," Mom said, getting up from the table and putting her plate in the refrigerator. It didn't escape me that she was leaving nearly half of her dinner on her plate.

"What else do we need?" My stomach felt heavy and twisted.

"Come here, Rylee." She wrapped me up in a gentle hug. "We're going to do something special when we get back, okay? I know you'll like it."

I was curious. "Is it boarding up the windows with plywood?" I couldn't figure out how we would do that on the second floor. You were supposed to secure the boards across the windows on the outside. I wasn't feeling too confident about this news.

"No. We really can't board them up, but we're going to be safe. I know it," she confirmed. "I just want to try to avoid the rush, so then we'll be home early enough to do something special."

We joined the rest of the people in the store who had waited until the last minute to buy their hurricane supplies. We were able to get some of the rapidly disappearing bottled water, cans of soup, jars of peanut butter, loaves of bread, flashlights, packs of batteries, candles, and storage bags. The shelves were quickly becoming bare, even though it was a big store.

Everyone near us in the long checkout line was talking about the hurricane. "Charley's forward speed has increased way more than they expected. They never know for sure!" A man was talking to a young couple in front of us, who had a baby with cute feet. "We'll get the next update in an hour, but I guarantee that it'll be a category three before tomorrow."

Experts were suddenly everywhere. I was facing the challenge of not becoming fearful.

"We'll be just fine, sweetheart," Mom whispered. "Don't worry."

We made it through the checkout, and then we followed a mass of brisk shoppers out the door. There was a different feeling in the air. People seemed anxious as they quickly loaded everything into their vehicles and hurried away on their next errand. We stopped by the bank to use the cash machine, and Mom took out forty dollars. We were able to fill up our car's gas tank after waiting in another long line. The news on the radio said that home improvement stores were almost out of hurricane supplies, and hundreds of people were waiting hours in line just to get inside.

It was like being told that the Big Bad Wolf was coming, and you needed to choose what kind of house you were going to build. Some people were driving through town with a couple sheets of plywood strapped on top of their vehicles. Several pick-up trucks were loaded with many supplies like packs of blue tarps, generators, coolers, chain saws, and more plywood. We saw a man at the gas station filling up at least ten red gas containers while we were waiting for our turn. I thought we might be underprepared, but I didn't want to say anything to my mom because I knew we couldn't afford to buy much.

She had let me get extra snacks at the store, so I was happy about that. I tried to distract myself by appreciating things. I walked around the apartment cuddling Mittens, while Mom finished organizing the supplies in the kitchen. I think Mittens noticed that I was nervous, because she didn't want me to hold her for very long.

I was pacing back and forth in the living room, but my mind kept going right back to thoughts about the giant storm that was on its way. Mom always told me to be aware of how I walked in the apartment, so the neighbors down below us wouldn't hear me stomping around. But the neighbors must have gone somewhere else, possibly a shelter. There were very few cars in the parking lot. Maybe we should have left, too. I went into the kitchen to ask for potato chips. I needed to crunch on something.

"Rylee, let's give Grandma a call and tell her that we're going to have a hurricane party." Mom smiled widely, handing me a bag of barbecue chips. "I already talked to Noah and Karin, so they know that we'll be just fine. I'm glad Noah went up to Tennessee with his dad."

I thought she might be going a little crazy. A hurricane party? There was nothing fun about it. "Well, okay," I said, looking forward to hearing Grandma's voice.

Mom finished talking to Grandma, telling her how we were prepared and not worried about the storm, that we were having this *party*, and then she handed me the phone.

"Hello, my dear."

"Hi, Grandma," I replied, trying to sound happier than I was feeling.

"Well, I believe that you might need to find an easier way to think about this storm, hmm? A party is a fine idea. Have fun! You know what to do."

"Yes, I know what to do. It's just kind of hard right now."

"I have some information for you. Hot off the press."

"Okay, good." She had all of my attention.

"This is an extension of lesson three. I know your imagination is in excellent form tonight, so here is what I'd like you to do in a few moments. Go outside and look around. Look at the nearby trees, their roots are deep in the ground and their branches are secure. They've already experienced harsh weather and survived many storms through the years. Put your hands on them and feel their great strength, expecting them to hang on tight. Imagine looking at them after the storm and how relieved you'll feel when they're still there, just as they are now.

"Stand back and take a good look at your home. Notice how the entire structure is built. It has a flawless design, enduring and solid. Think of the wonderful engineering and dedicated work that it took to lay the foundation into the earth. The sturdy walls will remain upright through any storm. The beautiful, supportive roof will keep you safe and dry every moment that you're inside.

"See the complete protection that is all around you. See it, feel it, know it, believe it. Not one doubt about it, Rylee. God will protect you if you will allow it. You just need to believe. That is one perfect structure that will be sheltering you every second of any storm ahead. Each certain thought about your safety allows God to provide you with it. Have faith that it will be so. God is right there, ready to assist you. You don't have to wonder how it will happen, because God will manage all the details."

I felt it already. I knew that we would be safe, without even going outside. Grandma just had to remind me how to do it, because fear had blocked my ability to think clearly. There was no doubt about it! I was eager to go outside, since she had asked me to, and I wanted to touch the trees.

"Thank you, thank you, thank you! Oh, Grandma, you really helped me! You make it so simple."

"No, darling. God has made it so simple. I just offered you a lift toward the high direction, a friendly little reminder."

While Mom and I were walking around outside, I looked across the field to the marsh where the edge of the lake began. I knew that the birds and other animals would find a safe place to get through the storm. The alligators would have to fend for themselves, though.

We stayed up very late that night and played games, never turning on the TV for a weather report, laughing wildly as we played charades toward the end of our evening. We would have time in the morning to learn anything else we might need to know. Our long hurricane party had begun. I realized later that my mom wanted me to be tired enough to fall asleep on the following night, the night when Charley came to town.

# CHAPTER 12

∞

HURRICANE CHARLEY WAS supposed to be a category two, possibly a category three storm by the time it made its projected landfall near Tampa. Many people evacuated the coastal area, some of them driving inland to Central Florida. But the fast-moving hurricane took an unexpected, abrupt turn to the east. It had also strengthened into a category four storm with winds up to one hundred fifty-five miles an hour.

We learned this news during an emergency weather update on our local news channel. When they showed an image of Hurricane Charley's new path, the swirling hurricane on the map was moving directly our way, right toward Osceola County. The eye of the hurricane rolled along, perfectly matching and covering our town's enormous lake. We knew that we were going to be in for quite a night. We were going to be taking a direct hit from the powerful storm.

The wind had been picking up all afternoon, seeming to come from many directions at once.

Before the rain began, we went outside and marveled at the pale yellow-green color of the sky. Dark clouds were appearing on the horizon, moving ever closer to us. There were many birds calling out, especially the blackbirds. They circled and screeched, never landing for long in any of the trees. They knew that something was coming. The air felt muffled, as if every sound had to push harder to get through.

We set up another party in my bedroom because it had the fewest windows. Mom and I dragged her mattress in and left it on the floor, where we would both be sleeping. She put extra pillows and all the couch cushions along the sides of the mattress. We arranged candles in several places on my dresser and nightstand, moving everything else into the drawers. I got to keep the biggest flashlight next to my pillow.

Mom put the batteries and lighters in sandwich bags and wedged them under her side of the mattress. The best part was all the snacks that we brought into my room: three kinds of chips, butter pretzels, chewy granola bars, and colorful packs of bubble gum. I was in junk food paradise.

Hurricane Charley was soon knocking on our door. The storm began to show its strength, howling and whining as it launched its attack. And then it quickly became a relentless force outside our home. The building trembled under the assault. When the electricity went out just after seven o'clock, it was suddenly as dark as midnight. I scrambled for the flashlight and Mom lit the candles.

"I think I'd like some chips now," I told her.

"Sure, go for it," she replied. "I'd like a piece of gum. Would you please hand me the regular kind, young keeper of the snack hearth?" We smiled at each other.

It sounded like cannons firing in the distance as power transformers began to explode. The nearby ones made us flinch when they boomed.

"Could those explosions cause fires?" I asked.

"Not likely, but if they did, the rain should put them out."

We brought the candles closer, so we could see each other better. I had to move slowly, so the wax wouldn't spill over as I moved my favorite, a lemon candle. It reminded me of Grandma and her lemon tea.

Mom briefly turned on the radio, trying to find a station with music, but most of them were giving hurricane-related news. The storm was roaring like an airplane coming in for a landing.

"Let me show you how to make a cool dog," she offered, taking a flashlight and patting my pillow. I settled down beside her. She held the light just right and made a dog shape with her hand. It seemed huge on the ceiling as she made it bark and growl. We amused ourselves for a while this way. I made the best duck. It even knew how to yodel.

Then we had a bubble-gum-blowing contest. Mom got a whole bunch stuck to her nose and cheeks when her biggest one popped. She had to borrow my piece of mushy gum to dab the sticky bits off her face.

"Do you want it back?" she asked, still laughing, holding the pink blob out to me.

I shook my head. "It's all yours now!" I reached over to pick out a new piece, watermelon this time.

We had enough light to play cards, so we started in on a game of gin rummy. I won twice in a row, once with all seven cards in the suit of hearts. Then I got out my shoot the moon game, where you try to make a metal ball roll up two inclined rods that you move around under the ball. We were both pretty good at it.

Mom collected older wooden games, which I always thought were the most fun. She was a madman with the cup and ball catching game. I just enjoyed watching her trying to beat her record. She'd make the ball slowly swing on its string like a pendulum, then she would swiftly move the cup, and the ball rose up, then dropped down right smack inside of it.

The eye of the hurricane closed in on us around ten o'clock. The roar of the storm got even louder, which didn't seem possible. We sat with our legs pressed together, leaning against the side of my bed and holding hands. The candlelight flickered, casting strange shadows on the walls. A memory entered my mind about the hurricane movie that Lisa had described to me. An image flashed into my mind's eye of our building breaking apart, and my mom and I being pulled out and thrown around by the angry hurricane. My bedroom suddenly felt too small and dark. I wished that I could turn on all the lights and walk around the apartment, but it wasn't possible.

"Rylee, if anything crazy starts to happen, I'm going to pull your mattress off the bed and hold it on top of us." Mom leaned over as she said this, then kissed my forehead, breathing in deeply. "The cell phone is in my right pocket," she spoke into my ear.

"Okay," I whispered. The real potential for something crazy to happen skittered into my worried mind, and my stomach clenched up. I wondered if we could suffocate in between the mattresses, how scary it would be if the building collapsed and we couldn't move to get out from under everything, pinned down by a wet mattress. There were sharp creaking sounds from somewhere up in the ceiling, and the wind was blowing so hard that the window rattled in its metal frame, letting through a fierce whistle like a hot kettle ready to explode. Everything was shuddering and shaking. I heard another loud sound and felt the impact as something else slammed into the building. It seemed as if a wild beast was determined to get inside, hungry and powerful on its mission.

The minutes were going by much too slowly. My whole body had tensed up, making my neck start to ache. I could tell that my mom was becoming more anxious. She seemed to be listening as hard as she could for a sign to make her move with the mattress. We had stopped speaking, because we really wouldn't have been able to hear one another anyway. I was feeling much too trapped.

I closed my eyes and took some deep breaths, trying to relax my body. With my eyes still closed, I chose to think about a favorite time at the beach.

It was a hot summer day with a warm breeze moving across the ocean. I remembered the gentle waves rolling in and out on that sunny day. My skin smelled like coconut from the sunscreen. A kind boy let me use his boogie board, and I learned how to ride the glistening waves all the way to the shore. I spent hours in the warm salt water, and by lunchtime I was very thirsty. I had to hurry across the hot sand to my towel, and the sand stuck to my wet feet like gritty socks. After a long drink of cool water, I ate my delicious sandwich. Seagulls floated down from the sky, bobbing their heads and inching closer to me. I wondered how their skinny feet could be on the hot sand for so long. I tried to toss pieces of bread crust to the smaller birds, but one of the big birds with speedy legs thought he was king. The chocolate chip cookies were soft and delicious in the warm sunshine. I couldn't wait to go back to the beach. It would be so much fun!

I realized that I was humming as I continued to relive every good memory I could summon.

Five more long hours into the storm, we heard a terrible cracking sound and the floor thumped and vibrated. Mom quickly turned and started pulling my mattress toward us. But when nothing else happened, she stopped, and then she held me close to her.

I took a deep breath, then I said, "I know we're safe. We are safe. We're safe at home." Our building was strong, and the trees in our yard had burrowed their roots deep into the earth. Their branches were secure. The animals had found good hiding spots. Mom and I would soon be sleeping comfortably under the perfect roof. We would wake up in the morning and eat breakfast in our safe apartment.

I envisioned all of this in my mind, and it allowed me to feel calm. I was certain that it would happen just as I imagined it. I was asking God to keep us safe, and I knew that my request was clear and consistent.

We did end up sleeping that night at some point, curled up together on our sides, harbored in the safety of our dreams. We had blown out the candles long before we settled in. By morning, the destructive storm had moved on to another place.

Charley was the strongest hurricane to make landfall in the United States since Hurricane Andrew in 1992. Charley took nine hours to cross the state and produced nine tornadoes along the way. There were thirty-five deaths and many injuries. Two million people lost electricity, and one-third of Florida's orange groves were destroyed.

When slices of sunlight came through the blinds Saturday morning, we awoke and went into the living room. Mittens trotted after us as we headed toward the front door to put our shoes on. She had been hiding under my bed all night. It was warm and stuffy in the apartment because the power was still out, so the light breeze felt almost cool on my skin as we started down the stairs.

"Oh, my gosh!" Mom exclaimed.

It was a different world. Several apartment buildings in our complex were damaged. Windows were shattered and blown out, and the roof of one building was missing large sections. Another building was partially crushed. An oak tree had fallen on top of half of it. My eyes didn't want to believe what they were seeing.

We walked around our building, carefully stepping over shingles, glass, and chunks of wood. Some of the paint was rubbed away and peeling off, and pieces of trim had fallen from around the windows, but there was no serious damage that we could see. The nearby trees were upright. Many branches were scattered on the ground, but none of the larger limbs had fallen.

We looked at each other, shaking our heads. Mom had tears in her eyes, and then my throat started feeling thick and full. I leaned on her as she put her arm around me. We had made it through the storm together.

She hugged me closer to her. "How about we go upstairs and open the windows to let in the morning air?"

"Okay. I want to check on the patio." I hoped we would still be able to sit outside. It was going to be awfully warm inside our second floor apartment without air conditioning. August was a blazing hot month in Florida.

We went inside and opened the windows, but the air still felt sticky. Mom started to put a fan in front of a window, but then she stopped in place. "Old habits die hard," she said, putting the fan back in the corner.

"What about the food in the fridge?" I asked. I knew that with the power off the cold things wouldn't last long.

"Only open the door when we need to get something out, and then make it quick," she told me.

I walked over to the sliding glass door that led to the patio. The chairs that we had tied together with rope were still there. We had flipped the table upside down before securing everything to the metal rails.

"Wait a minute, Rylee. Let me check it first," Mom offered. She looked left and right, then carefully stepped onto the patio. She peered over the sides of it and then bounced up and down. "Okay! We're good to go out here."

I was about to walk onto the patio with her when a loud scream pierced through the early morning hush.

"Where's that coming from?" Mom asked as she hurried to the front door and went outside, moving rapidly down the stairs.

I followed her. We heard a woman shouting, "Help! Please, help!"

The voice seemed to be coming from the apartment building with the tree on top of it.

"Hey!" Mom called out, walking quickly around the debris to the base of the building. "Are you okay? Where are you?"

A woman stuck her head out of a sliding door on the second floor of the building. The tree had fallen on the roof next to her apartment. "Help! My son's trapped, hurry!"

Mom dashed up the stairs, and the woman threw open the door. She was sweaty and her face was splotchy pink. I remembered seeing her before with a cute little boy in the parking lot.

"Quick, over here! The wall just caved in, and the bookcase fell!" she cried, getting down on the floor beside her son.

The boy was lying on his back. A tall wooden bookcase covered his body up to his chest. There were books scattered around him, some poking out from under the shelf. One of the wooden beams in the ceiling had fallen and pinned it in place. A large tree branch was right above the area, partially in the room.

"Let's get this off of him!" Mom said, bending over to test the weight of the shelf.

The woman shouted at the boy, "Ben, open your eyes!"

Mom glanced up at the ceiling. The tree branch seemed huge. It was resting on the other beams of wood. "If we can move this beam, we should be able to lift the shelf. You can slide him out then," she told the lady.

The woman appeared frozen in place as she looked at her cell phone. "I tried to call 911, but there's no signal!"

I could hear creaking sounds coming from above us. "We'd better hurry!" I said.

My mom pulled a chair over and stood on it. She reached above her and grabbed the long beam that had fallen on the back of the shelf. She tried to push it, but it didn't move. "Do you have a saw?" she asked.

"I've got a small one in the laundry room, hold on!" The woman ran down the hall and came back with a short saw that had a handle like a gun.

Mom looked down at the boy and then back up at the beam. "Okay, I'm going to cut this, then we'll move the shelf. Keep talking to him!"

"Okay!" the woman said. "Hurry! Ben, mommy's right here. Wake up!"

I didn't like to see my mom so close to the open ceiling and the tree. The wooden chair legs squished into the wet carpet, then started wobbling around when she began sawing. I grabbed the back of the chair to steady it.

"Mom, be careful!" I pleaded, worried she might get hurt. I stopped that frantic thought. Instead, I imagined the tree staying in place while we safely got the boy out.

She had sawed through half of the beam when it bent at the cut and snapped off, nearly hitting the woman. "Watch out!" the woman screamed. She moved her body to protect the boy's head.

Mom hopped down from the chair. "We need to lift it now!"

The woman stopped guarding her son, and we all pushed on the shelf, lifting it up a few inches, but it was still too heavy with all of the debris on it. I could hear more creaking from above us.

Mom cleared wet slabs of drywall and insulation off the back of the shelf.

"Okay, on three," she instructed. "We're going to lift together. Rylee, we'll need to keep holding it so she can get to him. One, two, three!" The shelf moved, and we got it up high enough to see the rest of his little body, which had some books on top of it. The woman let go of the shelf to reach for him, and suddenly it was too heavy for me to hold. It lowered back down, close to his body.

"Rylee, don't let go!" Mom yelled. "Push harder!"

It felt like my wrists were bending too far back, and it really hurt. I had two choices, and one was for me to keep myself safe. But I wanted him to live, so I shifted one of my feet closer to the shelf. I pushed up with my legs, keeping my elbows close to me. My body was quivering. We lifted the shelf high enough for the woman to push the books off of him. Then she slipped her hands under his shoulders.

"Hurry!" Mom groaned, straining to hold on.

It felt like fire was shooting through my arms.

The woman pulled him out of the way.

"Okay, Rylee!" Mom shouted. "Drop it!"

After we let go of the shelf, a loud cracking sound started above us. I felt like I was about to fall over as Mom nudged me toward the kitchen. I stumbled, trying to regain my balance, then Mom grabbed a handful of my shirt to keep me from going down. Another beam slammed onto the floor.

"Look out!" Mom warned, pulling me along beside her out of the living room. More of the ceiling collapsed as the big tree limb came all the way into the room. The wet leaves shook water on the damp carpet as the branches hit the floor.

The woman had moved her son into the kitchen and was crying over his body.

Mom brushed her hands off on her pants. "Please, let me see him," she requested. She leaned over, putting her ear next to his mouth while feeling his ribs and chest. She put three fingers along the side of his neck. "He's not breathing and there's no pulse. We need to do CPR. Do I have your permission?"

"Yes! Please save him!" The woman was clapping above him, saying, "Ben, wake up!"

Mom tilted his head back, held his nose shut, and put her mouth on his, breathing into him. She stopped, then carefully pushed on his chest many times with the heel of one hand. She went back to his mouth, breathing for him, then pushed on his chest. She kept doing cycles of CPR, then stopped and put her fingers on his neck.

"Come on, baby, come on," she murmured. "Pray, Rylee. Right now." She put her mouth back on his and continued her effort.

I imagined the boy starting to breathe and opening his eyes, as I said, "Please, God, help him. I know he's going to make it! He's healthy and strong."

Mom kept doing CPR, carefully re-positioning his head as she tried to revive him.

The woman was crying, "No, no, no! He can't die!"

Mom continued breathing for him. His small chest rose with her breath. She was counting out loud as she pushed on him.

She felt for his pulse again. "His heart's beating! Ben, breathe!" she shouted as she slapped the bottom of his bare foot.

The boy jerked a little, then he made a gagging sound. One of his eyes opened, then both. He blinked slowly, looking frightened as his awareness returned. He started to cough and whimper, then his face turned red.

"Ben!" his mom cried, laughing at the same time. "You're okay, you're okay!"

He lifted one trembling arm toward his mother. She leaned over and hugged him as he started crying in earnest.

"Oh, man," Mom said, wiping the sweat off her forehead and catching her breath.

The woman had her arms wrapped so fully around the boy that I wondered if he could breathe well enough, but he kept on crying. She lifted him up into her embrace.

"That is the best sound I've ever heard," Mom declared.

"You did it, Mom!" I said, patting her arm.

"Make sure he can move everything all right," Mom suggested.

"Here, baby," his mother said, lowering him to the floor. "Stand by me." The boy didn't want to let go of her, but he stood for a moment, then hopped up and down, trying to get back into her arms. "Okay, up you go," she said, lifting him to her.

She looked at my mom, and they gazed at each other, both of them with wet eyes.

"I can never thank you enough," the woman said. "Thank God you were here!" She put an arm around my mom, and they hugged with the boy in between them.

"You're welcome. I'm *so* glad he's okay," Mom replied. "You guys shouldn't stay in this apartment, though. You can come over to our place."

The woman agreed, so we quickly helped her gather a few things, and then we went up to our apartment. Mom checked out Ben more fully, using her stethoscope to listen to his heart and lungs, looking at his eyes with a flashlight, and feeling along his back, chest and ribs, but he seemed fine. His cheeks were still pink, and he laughed whenever his mom kissed his cute face. Ben finally let go of his mother after we had sat for a while in the living room.

I showed him my bedroom, and I let him play with my old toys and my favorite stuffed cat, one that I'd had since I was a baby. It was wonderful to see him busy being alive and wanting to play right away. Kathy and Ben ate peanut butter sandwiches with us for lunch, and we all laughed when Ben said he didn't like pushy trees. Mom and Kathy took turns reading books to everyone that afternoon. I gathered story books from a box in my closet, so Ben could enjoy looking at the pictures. He climbed onto my lap for a little while, still holding Lu Lu the stuffed cat under his arm. He even lifted it up and had it kiss my cheek. We all shared a snack, and then Ben took a long nap in my bed. They ended up staying overnight with us, sleeping together on our couch, cuddled up safe and sound.

The next morning, Kathy's sister made her way over to check on them, and they left to stay at her house. I let Ben keep Lu Lu, because he didn't want to let go of her.

Mom patted my back after we'd waved good-bye to them. "I couldn't have done it without you, Rylee. Thank you, again. You're very strong!"

"You're welcome. I'm so happy he's all right."

"Me, too!" she agreed. "How would you like to take a walk down to the lake? Let's go see how the birds are doing."

She took my hand as we headed down the street toward the lake, guiding me along as we stepped around the debris in the road. We saw cars with trees on top of them, and many of the houses had broken windows and torn up roofs. They were other people out, so we stopped to talk to a few of them. Everybody seemed rather shocked to be in the middle of all the destruction, but also, grateful to have survived. People that we had seen before but never talked to were coming up to us and being really friendly.

The damaged things all around us were only material possessions, items that might be fixed or replaced. What was important was being alive. I looked across the wide lake, its surface calm, reflecting the high blue sky. I closed my eyes and felt the warmth of the new day.

# CHAPTER 13

∞

NOTHING IN OUR town looked familiar for a long time after that windy night. People called it a war zone. Everywhere you looked there were battered homes and businesses. Yards were heaped with debris from damaged buildings and broken trees. We saw an entire roof sitting in a yard, and I hoped that Lisa and her family were all right. Fallen trees, especially the giant oaks, had crushed many buildings. The streets were nearly impossible to drive on because of the debris scattered everywhere and the mangled trees, their limbs tangled with a variety of shingles from countless roofs.

On the crackling AM radio stations, they told people to stay inside. There were electric power lines down, snaking across roads and winding through deep puddles of rain. When power was restored, the lines would become live and lethal.

It felt like we were living in a movie, a bad one that you're glad is finally over. But there was no way to change the channel. The devastation surrounded us on all sides for miles and miles, through every county in Central Florida and on both coasts where the storm had entered and exited.

It was almost completely silent in the midst of the destruction, because there were few cars on the streets, no stereos or TVs playing, no lawn mowers firing up, and no air conditioners kicking on. The first sounds to break the silence were police sirens and the droning buzz of chain saws, which went on for months. Streetlights were broken and hanging down, dangling on their frayed cables. Many telephone poles were blown completely away. The bright sunlight clearly exposed our unfamiliar town.

Power remained out during the hundred-degree heat. There were no stores or businesses open, so what we had to eat and drink was all that there was for us. We weren't supposed to drink the city water until the supply lines had been checked for contamination. Perishable food began to spoil in homes, grocery stores, and restaurants. Ice was suddenly a luxury in short supply. A cold drink was a memory from another day.

Transportation of needed supplies would not resume for an unknown period, because delivery trucks were unable to reach our area. The regular phones were out, and our cell phone had no signal. The lines of communication had been reduced to shouting distance.

Mom and I relied on our portable radio for recovery information. I was getting a little tired of sticky peanut butter sandwiches in the heat for most of our meals, but I was very grateful that we were safe and had food and shelter. We met friendly neighbors who shared some of their water with us, because we didn't have enough to last until the city water became available. They gave us eight gallons, a gift of liquid life.

The radio also reported that there were outbreaks of looting and violence, primarily in the larger cities. People were stealing what they needed to survive, and taking advantage of the stores that had been torn open by the storm.

I was thankful that we had been spared, even our old car. Mom wouldn't be able to go back to work until the roads were cleared and safe for travel. She wanted to call in to work, whenever the agency was up and running again, to find out how her patients were doing. The children she worked with depended on ventilators to breathe, and their back-up batteries only lasted for one afternoon.

Charley was good practice for us, because Hurricane Frances arrived twenty-three days later, September fifth, blasting right through Osceola County again. Fifteen inches of rain fell across Central Florida during the twenty-four hours that it took slow-moving Frances to cross the state. Those without tarps or plywood for their damaged homes experienced more destruction. Central Florida had only just begun to recover from Charley when Frances hit us. Some people had to start over with renovations, but Saint Cloud was not damaged as extensively by Frances as it had been by Charley.

And then the next one came twenty-one days later. Hurricane Jeanne played with us during a time when we were in a fragile state of mind. She remained out in the Atlantic Ocean just off the Florida coast for days. Then she made a turn to the east, which looked favorable; maybe it would stay out to sea. It took Jeanne two days to finish her complete loop to the right, and then she headed due west, straight toward the Florida east coast.

Jeanne decided to work her way right up the middle of Florida. The eye of the hurricane went directly through our county and it never left the peninsula until it finally crossed the state line into Georgia. The main route into Central Florida, Interstate seventy-five, was a path of destruction. Our state was in for a long recovery.

Supplies were few in the stores that had managed to open. Fuel trucks were unable to access our part of the state because of road closures, so people were hoarding gas. A rare gas station would briefly open, and then the long lines of vehicles would drain the available gas in one day. There was a sense of panic and disbelief throughout the region. Our normal way of living had ended.

Four major hurricanes hit Florida within a seven-week period. Hurricane Ivan, a category five storm at its peak, had slammed into the Florida Panhandle on September sixteenth, only eleven days after Frances. It seemed impossible that another one would come our way. The odds were against it, but then, you can't always predict the intense forces of nature.

I knew that we would be safe, and we were, through all the storms that year. Our building remained solid, and we managed to make it for weeks at a time on what little food and money we had, because my mom couldn't go back to work for a while after each storm. She had to stay with me when school was closed, and two of her patients' homes were damaged, so they had to relocate. Thankfully, all the children and their families escaped with no injuries. Lisa and her family also survived the storms, and they never lost their roof.

We received donations from Grandma Reilly, Grandpa, and Karin's family later that season. Mom cried with relief when their checks came in the mail. Her main concern after all the storms was that we might become homeless. Our car wasn't big enough for us to live in for very long. But we continued to survive and take care of our apartment, thanks to the loving generosity of others.

The day after a Christmas full of gratitude, Mom and I were shocked as we read the news report about the Indian Ocean tsunami. The earthquake that caused the tsunami was the second strongest earthquake ever recorded, and one of only five megathrust earthquakes ever documented. The effects of the Indian Ocean earthquake were noted all the way into Oklahoma, as the entire planet vibrated. The Earth's rotation was altered as it wobbled on its axis, and other strong earthquakes were triggered around the world, even as far away as Alaska. It was reported that the length of a day had been shortened by several micro-seconds.

So there was a way to change time after all.

Animals were seen fleeing for higher ground before the waves approached. Very few animal bodies were found after the disaster. It was quite valuable to be in tune with nature. We were still working on repairing our lives, recovering in Florida from our own monster season. My prayers went out far and wide to people I would never know.

In the aftermath of the destruction and desperation, we learned to be even more grateful. We were thankful for shelter, clean water, food, helpful neighbors, and workers who toiled into the night to restore our town.

I also learned that there might be situations that could shake your world to its very core, even an event that may seem impossible to live through. Yet, there is still a way to remain in a safe place, and a place to heal. The Source of love, of all creative energy, never ceases being available. People spoke of miracles and many acts of kindness because of the storms. Saint Cloud became a closer community after the hurricanes, as we slowly repaired our lives and beautiful town. It was clear how very much we rely upon one another for survival.

Those who lived through the stormy season were reminded that life is delicate, a gift to be appreciated. You don't want to dwell on the past, but there are some lessons there that may lead us higher.

# EPILOGUE

∞

THE NEW YEAR has just ushered in another clean slate, and I'm on winter break during high school. I've taken some time to write this down, because I believe it's important. Many things have changed since 2004, the year of those Florida hurricanes, but then, they always do. Nothing stays the same. That's the beauty of life: the diversity and the expansion.

Looking back on my childhood, I learned that when situations seemed challenging, those were the times when I developed tremendous inner strength. The year of the hurricanes stands out as the year that I began to take a closer look at the world, and I recognized that there were things I wished to see change. But I have learned that battling a person or a system does not support *lasting* change. To focus on destroying something can promote the continuation of it. Engaging with it in battle can often perpetuate it by feeding it with a similar fuel, which can drop someone down to that level and may attract matching energy back to them.

The belief that something holds any power, sends it power. Everything is energy.

Our consciousness energetically informs the object of our attention at the same level we witness it in, and that is the level we are met by it. It's more productive to learn what might work better and then focus on it, expecting that it will be so. We have the ability to lift everything to a higher way, because we can choose where to place our attention and how we hold anything in our witness. We can witness all in love, no matter how it appears. Love will then be restored everywhere, as it is the truth and the very fabric of all things.

Grandma Reilly told me that the old systems of control were ending, so the new may be born, but that it might not be apparent right away. I can now see evidence of this, as the systems that don't support *all* of humanity are beginning to fold under the weight of greed and domination. The heavy apple carts are tipping over, and the decaying fruit is being exposed. It may appear messy for a while, there may be disruption, but life can still be very enjoyable. We need to see what isn't working to no longer support it, or expect it. It might even be said that this is why we came here, which means that we have what it takes to see it through.

Last ditch campaigns to promote fear can be recognized for what they are: attempts to convince people to feel insecure, so that they might become submissive. But it is clear that we are so much stronger, and far less gullible, than is realized.

We are the home of the free and the brave.

The time is now to become a generation that stands firm, expecting what is beneficial for everyone. Nothing is more powerful than love, and the rising tide of love is flowing. The impact of someone witnessing anything in love begins to transform it, and the focus of many compassionate individuals will echo throughout all of time. Hold the line, knowing that all is well in the grand scheme of things.

We are the people—and united in love—we bring the power.

I've taken a jump way up high on top of my soap box. Grandma Reilly taught me this, and so very much more.

I shared the three lessons with my mom, and she learned how to communicate with God. At first, she was overwhelmed, because she would catch herself worrying or thinking negatively. But with more practice, and less attention to her slip-ups, she moved forward quickly. The Source of all things was just waiting patiently for her. It always takes practice to learn something new.

She is now involved in a charitable foundation, which was begun in honor of Brody. Her work is still helping people, but on a larger scale. She is very happy, and Aunt Karin comes to see us often because they work together. I sometimes hear them giggling, and then they'll laugh so hard that tears spill from their eyes.

Fay's little sister will be five this year. Grace loves to make Fay laugh, and they hold hands everywhere they go. I enjoy taking care of them while Mom and Karin do things like organize the charitable events and keep the foundation website updated. Noah and I both like to help them with the events. Noah does all the heavy lifting, because he's so strong. He's taller than my mom now, even though he's only in middle school. Mom likes to tell him that he is the finest man she has ever known.

I'll never forget the lessons that Grandma Reilly shared with me, and so, I wanted to share them with you. I haven't seen her since last year when we went to visit her.

As soon as we learned that she was scheduled for a heart procedure to implant a device to hold an artery open, we were scheduled for a flight to Iowa. Her doctor had recommended the procedure as an attempt to stop the dizziness that she had occasionally experienced.

Several days later, while Grandma was still recovering in the hospital, she had a heart attack on Mom's birthday. It happened during the first real break that my mom had allowed herself to take from Grandma's side. Mom wanted me to feel that we were doing something to celebrate her birthday, so we went to an afternoon movie. The show was quite touching, and I heard her quietly crying as we sat together in the dark room. Then Grandpa called, and he said to hurry. Mom drove like an ambulance on the way back to the hospital.

Grandma Reilly was now in the intensive care unit, her skin a pale gray, enduring severe pain while the doctor and nurses worked to revive her. Mom rushed in and leaned over the head of the bed. I stood by the door with Grandpa, because it was so chaotic. They told my mom that she needed to leave because they were going to insert a needle into Grandma's artery before her system shut down. Mom briskly told them to hurry up and do it, that she was a nurse, and that she wasn't leaving. The monitors were beeping loudly and alarms were going off. Mom spoke to Grandma and stroked her hair while they did the procedure, and Grandma heard her because her eyes opened wide and locked on Mom's.

Grandma struggled through the long night. She had chest pain and difficulty breathing. Mom stood next to the bed soothing her, never leaving her side, leaning down to press their cheeks together, and speaking softly to her. The staff told her to sit down and rest, but she remained at full attention, alerting the nurses immediately whenever Grandma's pain medication began to wear off.

When her doctor showed up in the morning for his rounds, Grandma was awake and sitting up in bed. Dr. Grittman couldn't even speak for a moment.

"Why, Miss Reilly," he finally said. "It's...nice to see you this morning." It was obvious that he hadn't expected her to live through the night. He had left the previous evening, shaking his head and telling us that there was nothing more he could do for her, that she was just old.

She replied, "Why, doctor, don't you know? It's hell to kill an Irishman." Even through her half-closed lids, you could still see the sparkle in her blue eyes.

Grandma was able to eat a few bites of the tasty things that Mom and I picked out for her in the cafeteria. Mom insisted that Grandma should have better food than the regular hospital food. They whispered to each other when Grandma was awake. We slept in her room that night, taking turns on a cot.

While Mom ran an errand the next morning, Grandma opened her eyes and moved her arm, drawing me closer. I had been holding her hand while Mom was gone because we wanted her to know that someone was always right there with her. I stood and leaned down so I could hear her better.

"Rylee, my love. My beautiful girl." Her voice was raspy from the oxygen that flowed continuously into her nose. "I'm ready. I want you to know this. Don't let your mom forget what she has learned. This may be very hard for her. She doesn't want me to go."

"Neither do I, Grandma! You might be okay, you know?"

"No, Rylee. I'm ready, and it's my time. I wouldn't mind staying longer, because life is so much fun. But I know I need to go now."

I was trying hard not to cry in front of her. "Grandma, *no*. I can't live without you!" And then I started sobbing.

"Oh, my sweet, sweet darling. Listen, you must always remember this: I'm not going far away. I'll be able to be near you anytime. Just know that I'm there. Help your mom with this, okay?" She was becoming weary from speaking.

"I will. I promise."

She looked into my eyes, holding the gaze. "Share what you know. With everyone. It's time."

"All right, I will." I kissed her hand and held it to my cheek. It was warm and soft. "I love you so much!"

"Rylee, you have made my life complete. I love you dearly, and it has been such a great pleasure."

"Oh, Grandma!" I leaned over and carefully hugged her. "The pleasure has been so very much... all mine." When she closed her eyes to rest a while, my tears seemed like they would never stop.

Mom was able to get Grandma released into hospice care the next day, so we could take her home to her apartment. She had said that she never wanted to die in a hospital. Dr. Grittman didn't want to discharge her, so Mom had to demand it with phone calls to his office every fifteen minutes, until he finally signed the order. A kind nurse helped arrange the ambulance ride to take Grandma back home, and we arrived just before sunset.

Grandma knew that she was back home. Unfortunately, her doctor neglected to prescribe the morphine that had continued to ease her chest pain after the heart attack. Mom was told that it would be provided, but that evening when the pain returned, we realized the morphine wasn't included in the pharmacy order. Mom paged the doctor, but he refused. He wouldn't allow Grandma any pain relief.

Mom was terribly upset, trying in vain to keep her comfortable, because she had promised her that she was going to take good care of her when we moved her home. It seemed an agonizing way to die. Grandma struggled through every breath, moaning and trembling on the bed. We stayed by her side, attempting to comfort her. It was like watching someone being tortured, but we couldn't stop it.

Mom had called the hospice office, and a nurse was bringing emergency pain relief, even though it was after midnight with snow falling in a heavy blanket of white. The nurse arrived twenty minutes after Grandma took her last breath.

Her passing was difficult to watch. I'd never seen anyone die. I waited for her next breath, holding my own, as her body let go of life. And then she was still. It was so final.

My mom was shaking as she cried, kneeling beside the bed. Her head was hanging down, her forehead resting on Grandma's shoulder. The loud machine continued to deliver oxygen through the tubing into her nose. Mom finally reached up and turned it off. I moved closer and put my arm around her, which made her cry even harder.

I remembered what Grandma had said, so I needed to let Mom know. I told her that Grandma would think of the painful time as a bad evening that was over now. But my mom was very distraught, completely focused on the unnecessary, painful way that Grandma had died. Grandma should have been allowed pain relief, but Mom felt it was her responsibility to ensure that the doctor fulfilled his obligation.

We waited all night, feeling drained and dazed, for the nurse and then the funeral home staff to arrive. We chose to leave the room while they prepared her body and put it into a black bag. They wheeled it on a stretcher, down the long hallway and into the cold night.

And then Mom began the phone calls. She was frozen in grief and anger, just functioning in a cloud of turmoil, so I wasn't able to get through to her. I knew that it was taking all her energy to make the calls to everyone who needed to know that Grandma had passed. She delivered the news, and then she tried to console each person as they reacted. She'd had very little sleep for days.

I looked around the apartment where I had enjoyed the delightful presence of my great-grandmother. She would never again need any of the things that remained: her eyeglasses, her water cup by the sink, her lavender bathrobe, her carefully folded dish towel, her crossword puzzle dictionary, and all of our family photographs on the wall. I felt an ache unlike anything I had ever experienced before. I missed her so much already. I wanted to see her smile and hug her one more time. How was I going to live without her? I started crying again.

But Grandma Reilly wasn't finished making sure that we were all right. The power of love is not blocked by the barrier of space or time.

A few days earlier, while we were getting food from the hospital cafeteria, Mom had told me that she wanted to tell Grandma her wish. She wanted Grandma to give her a sign from heaven, and she wanted it to be in the form of a blue jay, not to be confused with just any bird showing up. They used to take long nature walks together when she was a little girl, and they both loved birds. But Mom thought it was sort of goofy, and she didn't want to mention dying to Grandma, so she had never told her about this request.

As the bright sun was coming up the morning of her passing, we drove through the quiet streets to Grandpa's apartment. While we walked along the snow covered path to the door, Mom was ranting and raving about the negligent doctor. She wanted to sue him, or at least report him. She was intensely angry, saying that she hoped other elderly people were not going to be treated so inhumanely. It was a bitterly cold day, and the northern wind was blowing strong.

Suddenly, we heard a shrill screeching. It was loud and insistent, demanding our attention as we hurried toward the warmth of the building. Mom stopped, so I stood beside her, and we looked up to find the source.

Near the edge of the yard was a towering evergreen tree, its majestic branches moving with the wind. A blue jay sat on the tip of the very peak. The peak was swinging wildly around, but this bird was hanging on just fine, like a Christmas tree angel on a ride. I had never witnessed a bird so intent on being loud. The sound had to carry through the high wind and across the distance, but it had successfully interrupted Mom's recounting of Grandma's painful death.

Mom looked at me in a hopeful way as I said, "Do you suppose?"

"That would sure be nice," she sighed, but then she hurried on toward the door. The bird was still calling out.

It took over an hour in Grandpa's apartment to finish what we needed to do before leaving to go the funeral home. We selected photos and made other phone calls, and Grandpa had his morning shower.

Standing by the front window, we were slipping on our shoes as Mom finished telling Grandpa about the unnecessary pain that Grandma had experienced. She asked if he knew an attorney who could help her with a case against the doctor, because Grandma deserved to die with dignity, not drenched in pain.

Mom was becoming more upset, when the screeching started again. Only this time, it was ear piercing. A few feet from the window, on the closest limb of a maple tree, was the blue jay. It was actually looking in at us through the window, sounding angrier than any bird I had ever heard.

Grandpa said, "Well, that's odd. I haven't seen blue jays around here lately. And it's so loud!"

That's when Mom started laughing, slowly at first, and then she had tears running down her face. "Okay," she said. "Okay. I get it!" She was leaning over, slapping her hand on the back of the couch and snorting.

Grandpa was looking at her strangely, probably wondering if we were still going to leave. I linked my arm through his and said, "She'll explain it to you later."

We finally headed outside, pausing to look at the bird. It was hopping back and forth on the tree limb, invigorated by our presence, rather than being frightened away. It hurt our ears, being that close to it, so we moved along down the walkway as it continued sounding out.

The blue jay appeared eight hours after Grandma's last breath.

Mom never again mentioned any grim details of her passing after that winter day. Instead, she focuses on the beauty of her fine life, and we continue to share our favorite memories of her. We also enjoy lemon tea together, using Grandma's tea set, always pausing to lift our cups high and make many an Irish toast to her. I know she is smiling along with us.

And I imagine with all my might that every person, regardless of their age, gender, skin color, or nationality will be given the respect that they deserve in all situations. No doubt about it, life is precious to everyone. We are one world supported by God, moving into unity, with freedom and love for all.

It is comforting to appreciate the moments we've shared with those we love, because it provides one way to keep them close. But they don't just exist in the past. I know for certain that they are still nearby, eternally present in a place of pure love and joy, only one breath away, as we continue living here on Earth. If you pay attention, believe, and expect, you may see signs of their love all around you. They're waiting for you to open your eyes and know that they are here for you, if ever you want them to be.

Love never ends; it is the most powerful force in the universe.

And because you're reading this, I know that Brody and Grandma Reilly have touched another life. Here is their message for you, some good news to be reported. You are deeply loved and adored. You are always worthy, and you deserve joy. You are most powerful in love. You can always connect with God; it's your birthright. All you need to do is claim it, one thought at a time.

So tonight, I'll look up at the clear Florida sky and wish upon a special star, whose light shines on through the ages. I'll wish you every measure of peace and love in your lifetime, because I know that it really can come true. God is good, all the time.

∞ The beginning is here at the end ∞

# AFTERWORD: A LYRICAL PAUSE

— ∞ —

THERE IS A rhythm throughout the universe. The vibration throbs within every heart, during each moment of ecstasy, in every birth contraction. The rhythm exists in the pull of the ocean tide, around the weight of each raindrop, woven into every cocoon.

The sequence, the progression, is what we call time. Our time of influence affects the expansion of the universe. Heaven is eager to learn how we will add to the growth of eternal existence.

God is ready to respond as you take part in creation.

The rhythm never ends, it only strengthens and expands.

This life force is you. You are the mystery.

You are the journey. You are exquisite.

You are here.

Now, it's your time.

THE LIGHT OF compassion shined so steadily from within them that others could clearly see all the choices they were making, so they no longer existed in the dark. Without a word, without a sword, the energy that was void of light was unable to function on Earth.

This brilliant light, which emanated from individuals and became a collective force, stopped the planet's shifting.

The seas became calm.

The children stepped out to play.

And a new song was heard everywhere.

# Rylee's Notebook

$\infty$

**Patience**

Please remember that being patient will always help you enjoy life and not miss the good stuff while you're frustrated over something that's beyond your control.

**You decide**

You can make your own decision about God. I'm going to share what I believe, after years of studying, seeking, and praying. But you can find out what rings true and pure to you. Make your own decisions about all that you consider. As time goes by, you may even expand on what you believe as life reveals a new insight.

And you don't need to try to convince anyone that you're right and they're wrong. Your way of being is evidence of your belief. Everyone is different, because we're supposed to be. Would there be so many different types of people born if we're all supposed to be just the same? It may take some people more time to comprehend anything beyond the physical; necessary life experience might be needed for them to become receptive to spiritual information.

So please don't judge anyone on their individual path, or they will not experience your kindness. The smallest favor or grace shared with another, even a smile, may be a turning point in their life. And I want to share this information with you, because I love you. I certainly could have used this understanding when I was your age.

**How to begin**

You can investigate your mind and consider the way that you think.

What type of feeling does each thought create as it enters your mind? Notice that each thought has an emotion attached to it. As often as possible, continue noticing and evaluating your thoughts, remaining aware of the different emotions that go along with them. How easily does one type of thought lead to another that's similar? What happens when you start thinking about something that bothers you? And then listen to people, see if you can tell what their thoughts are focused on by what they're talking about.

If you're able to do this for a week, you will always know how to keep tabs on your thoughts. I know you're wondering about this. Just trust that it's a process you can learn step-by-step. This is all about connecting with God. Once you understand the process, you will realize how very simple it is.

## The high flow

You can move right into lesson two, which is all about how to feel peaceful and positive. A terrific way to distract yourself from negative thoughts is to look around, no matter where you are, breathe deeply, and then find something to appreciate: the shape of a tree, the soft blue of the sky, a beautiful song you remember, how helpful an escalator can be, anything. This will allow you to break away from any negativity that was brewing. It's also called "giving thanks," but you don't have to be down on your knees to do it.

Appreciating anything is being thankful. When you remain in a state of appreciation, you'll start noticing many things to appreciate. You are creating a peaceful set-point, no matter what is happening around you. This will become your point of attraction, this grateful state of being. You will open the door to a higher flow. Gratitude is a powerful energy. Let it flow. It's one of the quickest ways to bring more great things your way.

## One rung at a time

It may be challenging at times to find a better thought, like if you're feeling very sad. The remedy is to find a thought that's just a little bit better, even a grumpy thought. Those are better thoughts than extremely sad thoughts, only because you're gaining a little more control over how you're feeling, and then you don't feel as weak and hopeless.

If you can then make the necessary climb from anger to frustration, you will be able to reach a lighter feeling place each time you choose a different thought. Once you get to frustration you can move up to disappointment, and then you'll be even closer to feeling hopeful again. Just keep going. You can't always jump right up to a wonderful feeling place from a terrible feeling place. But you can always climb the ladder one rung at a time to a higher place, using your thoughts and intentions. As you practice and become more aware, you'll find that it just keeps getting easier. Asking God to assist you is beneficial as you move along upward. It would be helpful to claim out loud, "May I know myself in peace. I am knowing peace. I am in peace." Now that you're learning how to maintain your mindset, you'll never want to forget. It's the important second step to connecting with God.

**New pathways**

You will find that you become more skilled at it with daily practice. You're actually training your brain to develop new pathways. If you're ever faced with a big problem, even one that feels huge, you must not remain focused on the negative. You may work it around in your mind a bit, but if you can't find a productive thought about the subject, leave it. Use the distraction technique to find the best feeling thought that you can, about anything, even if it's only a tiny bit better. Because that better thought will be followed more easily by an even better one. You will make progress away from the negativity. If you get thrown off once in a while, not to worry. You know what to do, so just take charge again. No one and nothing else controls your mind but you. You choose how you want to feel in every single moment.

Nothing can *make* you feel a certain way unless you let it. You're the one choosing your thoughts. Don't be overwhelmed if you catch yourself worrying or thinking negatively. With more practice, and less attention to any slip-ups, you will move forward quickly. The Source of all things is just waiting patiently for you. It always takes practice to learn something new.

### Out of the old groove

People can develop habits of thinking and feeling, often from childhood, which they sometimes can't break free of as easily because those familiar pathways have been used for a long time. They may not know how to leave the old patterns of thinking behind. And when they start the bitter thinking, more negative thoughts follow right along, until they're nearly drowning in them. Then they look around and see how bad everything seems to be, and they call it proof that they were right in the first place.

This can create an odd kind of satisfaction, this apparent confirmation of the desire to be right, even about something negative. So there they will often stay. People can also get used to the habit of harsh thinking because it's a familiar way of operating. There can be a form of comfort found in anything familiar, even if it is not beneficial.

And life can be challenging when people frequently blame themselves. Guilt is like a bee sting, very painful when it first occurs, and then it causes a deep ache. It is also necessary to remove the stinger of guilt before it infects the body.

We can always learn from our mistakes, and then make different choices. Everyone has the right to do this. No need to keep holding on to guilt. You see, it's very important to know that you are worthy of being and worthy of love, no matter what you have *ever* done or thought. You are always worthy of love.

### Keeping it light

It's often beneficial to talk to someone, to reach out for help. But a problem can become more solidified if people continually share their sorrows. Then they keep the negativity alive, and it can grow into a heavier burden. When you speak about anything, it adds weight to the intention. You remind yourself of how bad you're feeling, and reinforce the idea of just how bad things seem to be, when you continue to think about it and tell others.

Life can present challenge and there may be discomfort or loss to rise up from, but you don't have to recreate your past by frequently focusing on it, dragging it right along with you. You can make a fresh choice in each and every moment.

**Just imagine**

Visualization is daydreaming with a purpose. When athletes want to perform in an optimal way, they often do it by thinking ahead. They take time imagining themselves going through the motions of their event in a fine manner. They go over it, visualizing it in their mind's eye, seeing and feeling the achievement of it before it even occurs. They remain positive about it, not worrying that they will fail. Then when they finally perform, they're usually successful.

A vivid imagination is a powerful tool. You may get what you are focused on. You may get what you expect. Label it any way you'd like, the result is the same. The reason is because every thought is actually a "prayer" in the sense that it is received by God.

**Beautiful and simple**

Understand that your thoughts are being received by the Source of all things. And know that what you think often determines what you will get. What you think, what you believe, is what you are matched up with, and you may then experience situations that match your expectations. When you think about something in a consistent way and believe that it might be, whether or not you want it to actually occur, it may take place because you are attracting it. Or something might happen that is similar to what you believe could be. It usually doesn't happen right away, which is why most people haven't recognized the process.

## No need to expect the worst

Many people spend a lot of time worrying. All the visualization that goes on in this case is done in a negative way. They spend time worrying about the possible ways that something could happen, dreading the idea of living it out, wondering what their friends would think, and gathering stories about others it has already happened to, even though they still hope that it won't occur. Their consistent focus and strong emotion on the subject increases the likelihood that this type of situation may become a reality. Without meaning to do it, they're expecting the worst.

## The big picture

God matches us with what we expect, what we believe. You will most often receive what you expect. God left it up to us to choose for ourselves, which is called free will. Everyone has free will and a creative consciousness. Your consciousness is your awareness. Your awareness is creative. Everyone is getting what they expect. It's been this way for all of time. We just haven't fully connected with the way that it works.

## The energetic fabric of the field

It works because of a principle based on magnetic force. The entire universe that God created relies on magnetic force to function every second. Even down to the tiniest of particles, the atom, where magnetic force keeps the electrons spinning in a harmonious manner. It keeps us physically alive. Every atom in each cell of our bodies must maintain this magnetic balance. And without the magnetic force of gravity, we would fly up into space, and the planets would not stay in orbit around the sun.

We're utilizing magnetic force every day in loads of inventions: telephones, televisions, clocks, tape recorders, and many more. Magnetic force is constantly at work, keeping our bodies, our world, and the entire universe in balance.

Our thoughts produce a strong energy signal, a magnetic request, that the field of God receives. We then experience situations that match what we requested. We magnetically attract what we expect, and it is reflected back to us in our daily lives. If someone believes that they will always be poor, they are expecting it. If they pray to God for help, but still hold the belief that they will likely never have what they require, they are still expecting to remain poor. They will get what they expect. Our free will allows us to choose. We attract, or get, what we expect.

**Magnetic power everywhere**

Have you ever played with magnets? Think about magnetic force. There is such power in the force that draws the two ends together. But can you see that force? No. It even goes through stuff. Solid stuff like a table! Put a magnet on top of a table and move another one underneath the table. It will look like the top one moves all by itself.

## The main signal

And when you try to stick the wrong ends together, it's impossible to do. You feel that if you try hard enough, you can mash them together, but the magnets will never touch one another. Such energy in metal rods, and in the universe! But the magnets only go together one way, just as God cannot connect you with something other than what you have magnetically attracted by your expectation. It does not fit in with the plan that God has used, across the board, for our entire world and universe to function.

You attract what you are truly expecting. Your expectation is the main signal that is being recognized by God. Your most frequent thoughts, your ideas, and the emotions that are created by them build your belief system. Your beliefs hold your real expectations.

Your desires and spoken words are often changing moment to moment. But your belief system holds your real expectations, and those core beliefs are what you will attract, because you expect that they are so. And they may be so for you, if you continue holding on to them.

## Every second of now

Prayers are thoughts, and thoughts *are* prayers. God does not need ears to hear everyone, because our thoughts and emotions transmit the energy signal of our expectations every second. God will provide your true needs, but you must expect this, which means that you must believe it and be open to receive it, even if it happens differently than you thought it might. The Source of all things knows what you require for your highest growth more clearly than you do, and is ready to provide for you.

## Unlimited potential

You don't need to decide that things must happen in a specific way, because you could block something perfect that may arrive for you. If you remain open to unlimited potential, you will clear the deck for wonder, wonderful happenings for you.

You can know that your true needs are coming to you, because that's what believing really is—it's knowing. Knowing is also having faith. You get what you expect, so you can choose to believe that your needs will be met in the highest way for your growth. God wants you to experience your life in the most beneficial way, so you can expect that this will be so.

God's system, the same one applied to the creation of everything in the universe, operates in this fair, consistent way. God loves us, God is love, and this is a perfect plan for everyone. We are so very cared for, and we get to choose. Are you still with me?

## More than three wishes

What we believe is what we're expecting *and* requesting, which can be different than what we're hoping to receive. And if we get to choose through our expectations, then whatever happens to us usually happens because we're expecting something like it.

Being this accountable can be challenging for people to accept. It might seem easier to blame someone or something else for unwanted situations, even our own past. Then people often hope that a few prayers during the week might keep everything in balance, but the world is not yet a peaceful place. Most of all, people are not living in the fulfilling way that they could be living on a daily basis.

We may not be able to reach the entire world right away, but we can certainly enjoy our lives, knowing how it all consistently operates in each and every moment. You get way more than three wishes, my dear.

## Thoughts can assist others

It would be good for you to listen to this a few more times, because I want you to absorb it so it will stay with you. And I will simply know that this is going to sink in fully for you. I will imagine you completely understanding all of this, which is part of the system. You can help other people by holding supportive thoughts about them. Your thoughts can actually assist others.

## Individual realities

Some people have had extreme challenge. Because of their experiences, they believe that the world is full of danger. And since they are powerful co-creators, just as we all are, their world has been full of danger. Share your beliefs a little at a time, knowing that they may need to hear it slowly. If you present it all at once, they might become closed off because others may have attempted to control them.

## Careful with that boomerang

I understand that you're concerned for them, but you can choose to resist thoughts that promote a negative reality. Let your sympathy be in the form of support rather than worry. Worrying about them will match you up with more things that may worry you, just as being frustrated or angry at someone and thinking bad things about them may bring you more things that could frustrate or anger you. Angry thoughts can attract more situations that could bring out your anger, and worried thoughts can bring you more to worry about.

So instead of "poor person" think, "I sure love them!" or "They are feeling just fine." Then use your imagination to hold images of that beautiful person at peace. Believe it with all of your might, feeling the emotion now that you will feel as it comes true. You have the ability and power to help them, more than you could ever believe is possible.

## Way to go!

Time to gather it up.

**Lesson one**

Keep the direction of your thoughts flowing in a beneficial way. Your emotions are your reliable guide to doing this. Every thought creates an emotion within you. That emotion will let you know if the thought is worth continuing. Slow down enough to notice your feelings; it's well worth your time.

**Lesson two**

Feeling peaceful is important. So if a thought feels harmful, stop it. Or if you must, think it through quickly, looking for lighter ways to reflect on the subject to resolve it; otherwise, change to a better feeling subject. Don't stay there, wallowing in worry, sorrow, anger, guilt, and fear any longer than necessary, because an avalanche of negative thoughts gains momentum and attracts more of the same. Climb up the ladder, no matter what. These thoughts are received by the field of God. The Source of all things matches you up with what you're attracting. You can request another delicious helping of bliss or another rough helping of misery.

**Lesson three**

You get what you expect. God created a perfect system that functions throughout the entire universe, and this plan will allow you to rise to your highest potential. Each person gets to help co-create what they will experience and receive. You can believe that what you truly need is on its way, and then notice all the wonderful things around you in the meantime, appreciating God's perfect system in action every moment. Then leave the details up to God, because God ultimately knows your true needs. Something new may happen in a way that surprises you, even something beyond what you could ever imagine. Just let go and let God.

## Thoughts affect reality

You have to wonder why it's not more widely understood yet. Why don't more people know that their thoughts affect their reality? And imagine this, we're supposed to be able to do many more things, having been made in the likeness of God, the ultimate Creator.

So if we were made in God's likeness, then we should be extra good at being able to create things. Why don't more people know about it?

I believe the true teachings were never fully revealed, because dictators didn't want people to recognize their own power. Leaders often used the strategy of fear to keep people in line, so their rules would be followed. Messages of freedom and fulfillment did not fit in well with such a goal, so the full teachings were hidden by those who were seeking to rule and command.

And the potency of a powerful spiritual message can become obscured when groups of religious followers insist on proving their position. Many wars were started because of the desire to be right about spiritual beliefs. The message of love can be the focus, not the mission to show favored status.

## The rising tide of love

Individual peace is needed to achieve world peace, so one of the things that we're here to do is to help others experience a peaceful way of being. Because you're learning this now, you won't encounter some of the obstacles that people can run into, such as being taught that they have little control over their lives, and that there's only one way that is right, so they must figure it out before they die, or else they might suffer forever in hell. The do-or-die approach allows no room for true love and compassion. Oh, my dear, the world took a sharp turn and just kept on going.

I wish to see love clearing the muddle that was created by greed and domination. But there will be a breakthrough. There will be an amplification of love, so we shall now move on!

## Soulful growth

You will be pleased to find out that you will never stop learning. We get to learn and grow during every experience, making our way through all kinds of situations to the creation of new understanding. Your soul, the broader part of you, also learns and grows through your experiences here. You will *always* exist as an eternal being, so there really isn't a big rush to get it all done. There will always be more to experience in life, so take time to relish the ride. You will learn from each experience and then go forward with more knowledge of what to do differently on the next go-round.

## Let it go

And you are forgiven, if you will also forgive others. This doesn't mean that you agree with what someone did. People can sometimes do harmful things, but you don't have to let it keep you in its grip. Without forgiveness, you can dwell in negative emotion, attracting even more of what you don't want. It's a vicious cycle. You're hurting yourself when you choose not to forgive. If you don't forgive others, you might remain in a place of judgment or anger, which may bring negative events into your life. And you must also forgive yourself, so you can move on without the ache of guilt.

## Land of choice

What you choose to focus on and believe will often be what is provided for you. To focus on the lack of anything that you require will likely keep it away from you. It can create more evidence of lack in your reality. And if you frequently complain, you could attract more situations to complain about. If you believe that the world is a dangerous place, it may appear that way for you. Whatever you focus on, you're inviting into your world.

**Powerful feelings**

It is more beneficial to choose thoughts that allow you to feel eagerness, love, and appreciation. Get excited about something that you're looking forward to, even something basic like a snack or seeing a friend. When those powerful feelings begin, let your mind choose more wonderful thoughts, which will allow the fine feelings to grow and expand. Let those feelings flow through you for as long as possible. More situations will come along that provide a way for you to continue feeling eager, loving, and appreciative. If you get goose bumps, then you're likely beginning to feel the energy of the higher vibration.

**The energy is real**

When you're not chilly, goose bumps often indicate that you're allowing Divine energy to flow through you. It's real energy. Everything is energy.

**Always in motion**

Our bodies are made of atoms, and there's a spinning magnetic field within every atom. We are truly made of energy. And our thoughts are energy signals, magnetically attracting matching energy back to us. It's all coming together now.

We are actually energy. And everything is energy. Imagine a computer screen that shows a strong energy wave flowing, peaking high and dropping low along with your thoughts.

## A system for everyone

Each step in this communication process can be understood so you may make a full connection. And the system that God so lovingly created for us is available to *everyone* on the planet. No one is excluded from the power of God's perfectly designed system, just as nothing in the universe is excluded from the power of the magnetic force of gravity.

## The rights were never for sale

Many people and groups of people have fought about the human idea of spiritual ownership. No one owns the rights to God's system—it just is. God is the energy of all existence. God is the fabric of all things. God is conscious awareness as pure love. Some people choose to join a group that claims to be the only one being cared for by God, as if God shouldn't take care of everyone else. If someone believes that they have the right to exist in a heavenly realm, yet they also believe that they are right to maintain the idea that others will perish and suffer, how is that of God? It is not. It is the very height of judgment. There is no love within that belief, only judgment that breeds conflict.

The world moved so far away from the messages of peace and love that it became a war over rights. The earlier messages were given to show the way, the way to connect, not to transfer ownership of the system. People tend to stake their claim on things, but God's system does not have transferable rights.

## The invitation

The field of God always responds to *everyone's* expectations, every moment, every day. And everyone is most assuredly invited to the party. Whether or not they accept the invitation to rise to the occasion is up to them.

We can decide to accept our differences, as we each grow at an individual pace. Just as you need not punish yourself because of your past actions, so you must not judge another as they grow and develop. All the children in the sandbox must get along. It's time to drop the swords and recognize how close we have come to the brink of disaster.

## Without end

But we will not experience a final "doomsday" scenario that ends our species, nor will we be over-taken by a group of dictators, because humanity at a higher level, a collective soul level, has chosen to realize the truth of our being, which is in unity with *all* of creation. We are finally moving beyond the idea of separation, the idea that God exists somewhere else, and that we are not one with Source, or with one another. We are now moving into unity. People will soon have a deeper awareness of themselves and of one another.

Everyone and everything is connected. It has always been so, but humanity chose to learn through the belief in separation. This belief was only an idea that was agreed to and perpetuated throughout the generations. It was never true. Nothing can be outside of God, unless we attempt to place it there by the belief that it is outside of God. This is how all fear and the idea of lack were created.

## Clean up on aisle seven

Humanity has done this on a massive scale, individually and collectively. Everyone is responsible for their creations, including a species. As we move beyond the idea of separation, we will be reclaiming all that was placed outside of God due to our witnessing it as such. The impact of our conscious attention is *far* more potent than we have recognized. The presence of the Divine has been denied and concealed by humanity's core belief that it does not exist, or that it exists elsewhere. This experience of separation is the world that has been created.

## The truth of all matter

It is time to claim love everywhere, in everyone, no matter how outside of God it appears, or someone chooses to appear, for that is where love is needed most.

It doesn't mean that we agree with what someone is choosing to do, or that we need to give them a hug. Not at all. It is not even necessary to speak to them to do this. Instead, we are simply recognizing the truth of their being, which must be of God, because nothing can be outside of God. All is of Source, or nothing can exist. You are recognizing the Source of them, not how their personality is choosing to act. You just know that they are of love, of God, because it's actually impossible to not be of Source. But people may hold the belief that they are separate from God, or that God doesn't exist, which creates the experience of it. We get what we expect. We get what we believe.

**The look of love**

Your steady, loving perception informs them energetically, which helps to remind them of their connection, because they may have forgotten it. You are helping them to remember the truth of their being by recognizing them as of Divine love. This can also be done from far away, because words are not necessary for the energy to flow to them. Energy naturally rises when a higher vibration joins it. The more certainly you believe that the Divine is present, the more fully the presence of the Divine is revealed to you. This revelation is how the world is made new, as the rising tide of love flows higher.

**It was only an idea**

Humanity's choice to believe in the idea of separation created an opposite energy from the energy of love. It is this fear based "anti-energy" that is now being reclaimed in truth, in the true vibration of everything, which is love.

### Beyond history

It may not be obvious now, but this great shift is well underway. The old systems of control are ending, and fresh new ways are being born that will benefit *everyone*. We are making history now; it is not making us. We have the ability and the right to choose a much higher way to exist. Imagine if many people realized this and began to claim everything in love, how quickly do you think the new systems would be born?

### Tip the scale

That's the spirit, darling. *Nothing* can stop this shift. It's just a matter of how quickly humanity chooses to move forward into unity. Personalities can sometimes have their own agendas, as everyone moves forward at their own pace. Every single person makes a difference. And one loving individual may be the catalyst for the tipping point. A collective belief is most powerful.

### Bring it up

Imagine a peaceful future, then expect it. You are choosing a higher outcome for your children and grandchildren. We can choose to take care of one another, as we all take care of our Earth. Imagine this peaceful way to live and be loved. We *all* want to feel loved and appreciated, so just offer the same and it will come back to you a thousand fold.

## A united state of being

Once we unite in all of this new awareness, we will move forward rapidly to create a more peaceful planet. It is not only possible, it's right there, already set up and ready to go, only one thought away. And it would be so much fun!

There would be no more fear of losing your freedom. We would all know that we're responsible for our own lives, that we do have a hand in choosing our experiences. Circumstances don't fall from out of the clear blue sky into our reality. We've usually requested them by our expectations—those constant prayers. There would be no more reason for blame, no more judgment and condemnation.

We are all striving to exist and thrive, and we each have different challenges to meet. No one knows what someone else has come here to learn and experience. To stand in judgment of others may attract even more for you to judge harshly, and others who may judge you. The best way to live is to love everyone, no matter what. You then attract those who will love you, no matter what.

## No time

And all of your creative power is in the present moment. Right now. There's no time like the present. The past is over, and the future never arrives, so remain present. Nothing else is happening, but what is happening right now. The past and the future are now just ideas. It is always right now. Our minds sure like to go fishing around in the past, or trying to reel in the future.

## On a peaceful path

Each of us is unique, but we are all from the same Source. Many different journeys will lead to a new awareness of God; some are short and straight, while others are long and winding. We can stay on our own path, being an example, and allow our brothers and sisters their chosen travels. Do not be a thorn on anyone's path. Plant the seed of love, and the elements will support the flowering of peace as it blooms. Even if a flower wilts, its sweet fragrance is still released into the world.

## Wildest dreams

This heightened understanding will lead to peace for families and countries and eventually the entire world. Maybe in your lifetime. There will be no more arguing about who should own the rights to God's love. We are *all* eternal beings, recognized by God, every single one of us. God's system of fulfillment is available to every human, without exception. What each of us chooses to do with our free will is simply up to us.

The kingdom of God, the awareness of the Divine in all things, is truly within you, awaiting your agreement to it. Connect with it, and you will experience life beyond your wildest dreams.

## Keeping the balance

You may prevent disease by making this connection with God. Put the three lessons into action, and you will feel the balance in your body, mind, and spirit. Stay connected, and good health may be yours because you will not be stuck in fear, anger, guilt or sadness for any length of time.

Do not focus on, or fear, an illness. No entertaining any thoughts of what you do not want. Just imagine your body being strong and healthy, no matter what. Even if you have symptoms of something, take control. Natural remedies and good medical care can assist you in healing, but the way that you think has an absolute effect on your body.

And laughter really is good medicine, so have fun! It's important for your entire being. All the chemicals and hormones released when you smile and laugh strengthen your immune system more than any drug we could ever invent, not to mention how good it feels!

## Hello, beautiful

And love yourself, as God loves you, unconditionally. Enjoy who you are without feeling the need to change your hair, your job, and your clothes before you will finally be satisfied. You're already so beautiful! You can feel content right where you are now, even if you desire something other. The Source of all things wants you to receive what you truly need, so don't block it by focusing on the absence of anything. It's very beneficial to feel appreciation and pleasure within your current state of existence. Grateful thoughts are powerful.

## Time to rise

There may be people who continue to step on their own feet, but for those people we can still send our supportive thoughts, continue living out our example, and wish them the best. Some people don't realize that they're choosing to feel bad, because they've never escaped the past, those habits of sour thinking about negative memories. Then they often dread, and continue to receive, more of the same. It requires new movement to break free from the past; one thought at a time *up* the ladder, as you leave the past where it belongs. When a person decides to rise, they'll quickly notice the fine results of this choice.

## Pack a parachute

You may also do your part by moderating your habits. You can't jump out of an airplane and expect to land softly just because you've imagined it as you're falling. Listen to your intuition—God is trying to tell you something.

## We're all in this together

And love others, as you love yourself. When you give, in thought or deed, you actually receive. The well flows even higher for you when you share. To help another, even by focusing on a supportive thought for them, may also attract and bring you support, and it could come about right when you need it. The people you help may wish you well for your assistance, and then they might be more inclined to help someone else, and on and on.

Once you've experienced it, and you feel the pure connection, it's the only way to live. There's no going back. You can't let yourself, because you know how God's system operates.

## Constant awareness

What we expect from other people is usually what we get, or attract, from them. When we want someone to change, or to stop behaving a certain way, we often continue thinking about how much their behavior upsets us. If we continue to focus on the person's negative behavior, we can only attract what we're expecting from them. God's system applies to everything: to atoms, to our bodies, to nature, to gravity, to our journey around the sun each year, to God's constant awareness of what we're expecting.

So, an effective way to help a person is to imagine them being well; visualize them healthy and strong, peaceful and content, whatever it is that might assist them. You're not trying to fix them to be the way that *you* want them to be. You're simply remaining positive in your own thoughts about them, allowing your witness, your focus on them, to lift them. We can help one another this way. Being angry at them only attracts more from them that may cause you to experience anger. Appreciate them, and they will likely show you more to appreciate.

## The set-point of love

It just follows along with the same principle. Now imagine how it would be if you chose to witness everything in love, no matter what was happening around you. What do you think would come your way?

## Eternal melody

My love, many souls do not need a lot of time on Earth. In heaven there is no time. They probably enjoyed everything to the utmost while they were here. There is no true death, no final ending to existence. There is only a transition, a change. We will *always* continue to exist. And no one caused their death by worrying about them being hurt or dying. No one made it happen. If our thoughts could kill someone, people wouldn't need to use weapons in war, and I wouldn't want to drive in rush hour traffic.

There is a rhyme and reason to the way that souls flow in and out of physical life. We will understand it later. You will be together again, and they know this. It may be difficult for you to live on without them physically here, until you understand that right now they are more fully alive and aware than they have ever been. They are part of the greatest love song ever imagined.

**They even come to dance**

You see, many souls come here for only a short time. They come for important lessons and to bring their love here. Quality of life is not measured by quantity of years. They may have lived more fully than someone who has lived eighty years. Just know that all is well. God's energy never ceases being available to you, not even for one second.

**Forever present**

It is comforting to appreciate the moments we've shared with those we love, because it provides one way to keep them close. But they don't just exist in the past. I know for certain that they are still nearby, eternally present in a place of pure love and joy, only one breath away, as we continue living here on Earth. If you pay attention, believe, and expect, you may see signs of their love all around you. They're waiting for you to open your eyes and know that they are here for you, if ever you want them to be.

Love never ends; it is the most powerful force in the universe.

**Safe and sound**

I know your imagination is in excellent form, so here is what I'd like you to do in a few moments. Go outside and look around. Look at the nearby trees, their roots are deep in the ground and their branches are secure. They've already experienced harsh weather and survived many storms through the years. Put your hands on them and feel their great strength, expecting them to hang on tight. Imagine looking at them after the storm and how relieved you'll feel when they're still there, just as they are now.

Stand back and take a good look at your home. Notice how the entire structure is built. It has a flawless design, enduring and solid. Think of the wonderful engineering and dedicated work that it took to lay the foundation into the earth. The sturdy walls will remain upright through any storm. The beautiful, supportive roof will keep you safe and dry every moment.

See the complete protection that is all around you. See it, feel it, know it, believe it. Not one doubt about it. God will protect you if you will allow it. You just need to believe. That is one perfect structure that will be sheltering you every second of any storm ahead. Each certain thought about your safety allows God to provide you with it. Have faith that it will be so. God is right there, ready to assist you. You don't have to wonder how it will happen, because God will manage all the details.

**Come in unity**

There might be situations that could shake your world to its very core, even an event that may seem impossible to live through. Yet, there is still a way to remain in a safe place, and a place to heal. The Source of love, of all creative energy, never ceases being available. There will be miracles and many acts of kindness. Become a closer community after any storm, and you will repair your lives and beautiful families. It's clear how very much we rely upon one another for survival.

Those who live through a stormy season are reminded that life is delicate, a gift to be appreciated. You don't want to dwell on the past, but there are some lessons there that may lead us higher.

### No need for a battle cry

When any situation seems challenging, those are the times when you may develop tremendous inner strength. If you take a closer look at the world, you may recognize that there are things you wish to see change. But you may learn that battling a person or a system does not support *lasting* change. To focus on destroying something can promote the continuation of it. Engaging with it in battle can often perpetuate it by feeding it with a similar fuel, which can drop someone down to that level and may attract matching energy back to them.

### Keep the charge

The belief that something holds any power, sends it power. Everything is energy.

### Level up

Our consciousness energetically informs the object of our attention at the same level we witness it in, and that is the level we are met by it. It's more productive to learn what might work better and then focus on it, expecting that it will be so. We have the ability to lift everything to a higher way, because we can choose where to place our attention and how we hold anything in our witness. We can witness all in love, no matter how it appears. Love will then be restored everywhere, as it is the truth and the very fabric of all things.

## The great shift

The old systems of control are ending, so the new may be born. We can now see evidence of this, as the systems that don't support *all* of humanity are beginning to fold under the weight of greed and domination. The heavy apple carts are tipping over, and the decaying fruit is being exposed. It may appear messy for a while, there may be disruption, but life can still be very enjoyable. We need to see what isn't working to no longer support it, or expect it. It might even be said that this is why we came here, which means that we have what it takes to see it through.

## Turn off that program

Last ditch campaigns to promote fear can be recognized for what they are: attempts to convince people to feel insecure, so that they might become submissive. But it is clear that we are so much stronger, and far less gullible, than is realized.

We are the home of the free and the brave.

## Hold the line

The time is now to become a generation that stands firm, expecting what is beneficial for everyone. Nothing is more powerful than love, and the rising tide of love is flowing. The impact of someone witnessing anything in love begins to transform it, and the focus of many compassionate individuals will echo throughout all of time. Hold the line, knowing that all is well in the grand scheme of things.

## Great power

We are the people—and united in love—we bring the power.

## A high pledge

And imagine with all your might that every person, regardless of their age, gender, skin color, or nationality will be given the respect that they deserve in all situations. No doubt about it, life is precious to everyone. We are one world supported by God, moving into unity, with freedom and love for all.

## Love is alive

And because you're reading this, I know that Brody and Grandma Reilly have touched another life. Here is their message for you, some good news to be reported. You are deeply loved and adored. You are always worthy, and you deserve joy. You are most powerful in love. You can easily connect with God;

it's your birthright. All you need to do is claim it, one thought at a time.

## Star bright

So tonight, I'll look up at the clear Florida sky and wish upon a special star, whose light shines on through the ages. I'll wish you every measure of peace and love in your lifetime, because I know that it really can come true. God is good, all the time.

# ABOUT THE AUTHOR

— ∞ —

JULIE BARNES WORKED as a nurse for 20 years. *All Flavors* is her second novel. Her first novel, *From the Depths*, is a therapeutic thriller that introduces the characters in *All Flavors*. She is working on her next book.

Connect with her:
JBarnesAuthor.com